I

Figment

FIGMENT

C. W. Johnston

Figment

Copyright ©2020 by C. W. Johnston
Cover design by C. W. Johnston and Michelle Fairbanks
Book design and production by C. W. Johnston, www.cwjohnston.com
Editing by Kate Schomaker
Photograph on cover by Frances Perles (used by permission from Unsplash)
The Lyrics from *K-K-K-Katey* on page 189 are by Geoffrey O'Hara
The song *This Train* (origins are unknown)

To my daughter, Emily

For your enthusiasm and belief. Without you there would be no book.

Figment

PART ONE

Figment

CHAPTER ONE

His Jeep shuddered around the treacherous turns of the logging road that led further into the Bitterroot Mountains. He knew this route well. Like the crevasses and holds of his favorite climbs, this road had a feel—a way to leverage an advantage and nuance it with each sudden brake and frenetic spin of the steering wheel. His vehicle barely gripped the surface as the engine screamed and his tires spun at the loose dirt, machine-gunning the dense foliage on either side of him.

Tyler Stevens was in his element. It was the weekend; the top was down on his aging convertible Jeep, and he was a ready and willing participant in this weekly wilderness adventure.

Whatever the season, Tyler was first in line. In the late spring and summer, it was kite surfing, spelunking, mountain biking, and rock climbing. Telemark skiing ruled the winter unless he felt the urge to head south to the Bahamas to dive and spearfish. This was his world. As his friends would tease, he was compelled to be "fully engaged in life."

On the weekdays, Tyler was an above-average sociology professor at a less-than-average liberal arts college nestled in a sleepy valley in western Montana. The new college in Missoula served as a gateway to his passions—full stop. The location, not the job, lured him west from Michigan. Had he pushed for it, he might have been nicely set up at a more prestigious institution—one that people may have even heard of—but it wasn't what he wanted. Out here, beyond the din and the meaningless self-importance of city life, was where he felt most alive.

Athletic and "outdoorsy handsome," Tyler was thirty-two and still single. Partly because he was a little shy around women, but mostly because he was too busy with teaching or conquering the next peak to do anything about it. Women were interested in Professor Stevens, but most of the time he was oblivious to their flirting. As soon as his Friday lectures ended, he could be seen running down hallways, pushing through the doors, and almost flying down to the staff parking lot. Effortlessly hopping into his red Wrangler and racing past the college gates, he was determined to get up into the mountains before sundown.

Today he had turned off Highway 90 an hour after leaving campus and headed into the mountains by way of various abandoned logging roads. It was a warm, beautiful afternoon, and the fresh mountain air ripped through his longish brown hair. He felt alive. He smiled and turned the radio up. Don Henley was belting out "Boys of Summer." Life was good.

After four miles of semi-recognizable road, he headed up an old dirt logging trail that he had visited on occasion. The mountains were right above him now, ominous and towering. Tyler slowed down, pulling his stick shift back to its lowest gear. He turned left sharply onto a barely visible, overgrown jammer road created in the 1950s for loggers to haul timber up the steep hillsides. After years of scouting the area, Tyler knew this one was relatively easy to negotiate. Nimbly avoiding the alder and pines that were beginning to reclaim the narrow space, he navigated the bumpy terrain with precision.

The various mountain ranges that encircled Missoula each offered their different challenges. Today he wanted to explore farther up the incline than he had ventured previously. The topographical map showed there was a remote pond with a possible vista about five miles from where he was—Whisper Ridge, so named by the indigenous people in the area. On Google Earth, he could make out the narrow shelf clinging between two steep inclines. From what he could gather, it had never been logged or explored. It was a thin ridge, perhaps one hundred meters wide, that led down to a tiny valley.

Not much, but it was something new.

It was late afternoon, and he wanted to set up camp before dark. At the end of the jammer road, Tyler found another connecting side path, just wide enough for him to maneuver his way carefully through the menacing branches. He didn't mind the scratches on the side of his Jeep. They were character building.

He knew remnants of the next jammer road would be about sixty feet to the north, the standard distance between these types of passageways. Tyler had to duck as the heavy branches pulled over his windshield and released, whip-like, above him. After eventually arriving at a clearing where the road suddenly ended, he parked the Jeep and hopped out, looking up the steep embankment he was about to ascend. He took a swig of water, threw on his large backpack, checked his compass, took a deep breath, and headed into the dense foliage.

After a few hours and an exhausting, steep scramble through the forest, the terrain began to flatten out, and the trees soon gave way to saplings and then finally some meadow grass. He headed north, finding and following a deer trail. Eventually, he came to a small bluff; climbing to the top, he stopped and smiled.

Below him was a pond—less than 150 meters in circumference—and beyond it a sweeping valley looking back over the Reservation Divide Range in the distance. Wildflowers dotted the grass on either side of the shimmering water. He clambered down to the shore and found a large log, dropping his heavy pack beside it. He would pitch his tent here. It was perfect.

He spent the next forty-five minutes preparing his campsite and then walking around the small pond, taking pictures with his cell phone. Once home with access to the internet, he would upload them to his Instagram account—a collection of images of flora, fauna, and vistas found in the area. He found immense satisfaction in looking back at his photos, though his actual followers were few and far between.

The pink dusk had given the wildflowers a translucent glaze that drew him to capture the moment. He climbed the small embankment on the far side of the pond to look into the darkening valley below, watching the day's last light reflect off the top of the peaks before disappearing. He headed back to his campsite to light his fire and make dinner.

By the time he had finished eating, it was almost dark, and Tyler sat back, fully satisfied. It had been a long week of teaching, and he was bushed. He was now in a state of meditative peace; he drank in the fresh mountain air of the encroaching night.

As was his custom on these kinds of adventures, Tyler pulled out his trusty harmonica, a classic Hohner Marine Band ten-hole harp. They only had a few tunes in common, but it gave Tyler great comfort to finish off the night with his harp. It was his traveling companion; it helped him find solace in storms, calm in precarious situations, and even company when lonely.

He wasn't sure how it became one of his favorites, but "This Train Is Bound for Glory," the old American gospel song from the early 1900s, resonated with him profoundly. Tyler took a deep breath and began to play. As often happened in the mountains when playing his harp, he could hear the coyotes in the distance howling in response.

The stars were in full force and his fire almost out when he finally crawled into his tent for the night.

It was 3:37 a.m. when his mobile alarm went off.

CHAPTER TWO

Tyler sat up, startled and disoriented. He never set his alarm, even at home. He must have pushed something by mistake. After turning the irritating sound off, Tyler snuggled back into the warm sleeping bag. He was drifting off when it sounded again, the light of his phone illuminating the interior of his small tent.

"Ugh," Tyler mumbled as he rolled over and grabbed his phone again, this time turning the power off completely and throwing the phone to the other side of the tent. He collapsed back into his sleeping bag, pulling it over his head. Sometimes technology baffled him.

It was when the alarm went off a third time that he felt the first chill run down his entire body. "What the—" he blurted out, leaning over to find the phone on the other side of the tent. When he finally found it, he switched off the alarm again and unlocked his phone to see what might be malfunctioning. He was wide awake now and breathing rapidly. He could hear the crickets returning to their chirping in the bushes behind the tent.

Confused, Tyler sat up and scrolled through the settings options. The alarm was well and truly off, but he waited to see if it would happen again, staring at his now quiet phone. There was no access to the internet in this remote area, so he opened up his photos icon to review the pictures he had taken earlier that evening. He shuffled through them until he saw something that made his blood run cold.

Tyler rubbed his eyes, attempting to wrap his head around the image in front of him. It was a photo he definitely had not taken. It was also a physical impossibility.

"*Jesus.*" Tyler's heart was pounding. He leaned forward, his senses on overload as he attempted to make sense of the image on his screen.

It was a picture of himself, taken earlier in the evening. He was sitting on the log by the fire, playing his harmonica. It had obviously been taken on his own phone—the same one that had been in his pocket the entire time.

Tyler felt his heart racing, and his temples were pounding; he instantly felt very much alone in this remote wilderness. Something he had never felt before.

It was beyond comprehension. Somebody had somehow taken a picture of him from the other side of the fire that evening. Whoever it was had used his phone, as the image had not been sent to him. It was in his camera roll. He could even see the time it had been taken—8:48 p.m.

But his phone had never left his pocket.

It suddenly dawned on Tyler that, regardless of how it happened, somebody might still be out there. Goose bumps shivered down Tyler's skin, and he immediately felt his survival instincts kick in. He cautiously crawled out of his sleeping bag, grabbed his flashlight, and unzipped the tent. As he stepped out into the chilly darkness, the bright moonlight allowed him to see well enough. Nonetheless, he turned on his flashlight and quickly pointed it in every direction.

Nothing.

Tyler walked over and sat on the same log where the picture of him had been taken and turned the flashlight off, listening for anything unusual.

Nothing.

It was now almost four in the morning. Tyler was almost panting, and he could feel his blood surging through his veins. Something definitely was not right. Turning on his flashlight again, he slowly scoured his surroundings and listened for any movement. All was deathly quiet.

After a few minutes, Tyler returned to his tent, secured the zipper, and reluctantly crawled back into his sleeping bag. There was nothing more he could think of to do but wait until daylight. Again, Tyler turned the power off on his cell phone, then stared at the ceiling of his tent. He knew he would not sleep any more that night.

*

At first light, Tyler took down his tent and hastily packed up his gear. His dream of a relaxing weekend camping had vanished. He was shaken and wanted to get out of there as soon as possible. He needed some perspective.

Within an hour he had scrambled back down to his Jeep. Scraped and bruised by the foliage, he quickly threw his pack onto the back seat. His hands were shaking as he immediately started the engine, managing to turn around in the narrow space. He slowly navigated his way back down the tight trail to the first jammer road. He was back on the highway heading to Missoula forty-five minutes later.

Trying to calm his mind, Tyler reached for the radio and switched it on to the local classic rock station. He needed a distraction. He recognized Fleetwood Mac. Something from *Rumours*.

And then it changed.

It took him a moment to realize the music he was listening to now sounded way too familiar. That sickening, pulsating feeling returned in his chest, and he felt nauseated. Tyler slammed on the brakes, the car swerving back and forth until he came to a jolting stop at the side of the road. He turned the radio up. It was harmonica music—his harmonica. He could just make out the coyotes howling in the background.

CHAPTER THREE

It was just after ten on Saturday morning when Tyler eventually clambered up the exterior stairs to his two-bedroom apartment overlooking the Rattlesnake Mountains on the edge of Missoula. Completely freaked out, he threw his keys on the table and dropped his backpack against the closet door while kicking off his boots. Tyler then made his way to the bathroom. He flicked on the lights, then leaned over the sink and stared into the mirror. *What the hell is going on?* He looked down at his hands; they were shaking uncontrollably. Tyler peeled off his clothes and stepped into the shower. He closed his eyes and let the hot water pound down his body.

The rest of the day he kept himself as busy as possible. No cell phones, no radio. He busied himself at the weekend market and then headed out to the park to watch some local kids play softball. Then he simply walked. He occupied his mind with what was happening around him. He tried to be near people, to hear their conversations, and to feel their presence, as if that would bring some normalcy to his confusion. He walked until he was too exhausted to go any further.

That evening, back at his apartment, he decided to order in pizza and watch the college football late game. USC was hosting his alma mater, the Wolverines. He opened up a beer and tried to relax, though he could not ignore the tense ball in his gut. At halftime, he went over to his cell phone in the kitchen, unplugged it from the wall, and robotically checked his emails, text messages, and the weather—trying not to dwell on the obvious. He then reluctantly opened up his camera roll.

Still there. FUCK.

The picture of him was clear and deliberate. It had been taken about twenty feet from the other side of the fire. *From that stand of alders*, he thought. He spread his fingers wider, enlarging the photo, and moved it around to see if there were any other clues, but there was nothing obvious. His stomach felt like exploding. It was impossible to comprehend.

By eleven thirty, he decided to call it a night. As anxious as he was, he was asleep within twenty minutes.

At first, he thought it was the car in his dream honking at him. Gradually, as he regained consciousness, he realized it was his cell phone ringing. It was still in the pocket of his jeans by the bed. He looked at the clock on his nightstand.

3:37 a.m.

He quickly put on the light and reached for his jeans and dug out the still ringing iPhone. His chest was throbbing again.

"Hello," he answered weakly.

Nothing.

"Who is this?" Tyler demanded as the call ended and the line went dead. He tried to call back, but the number was unavailable.

He had just put the phone down on his night table when it vibrated, indicating a text had come through. His hands were shaking as he picked up his cell phone again. The text message was only one line long:

This Train Is Bound for Glory.

*

Cynthia Chan had called Missoula home since she was ten. Her parents had moved there from Seattle. Like most folks who came to Montana from elsewhere, they were drawn by the lifestyle and the low cost of living. Cynthia eventually had gone back to Seattle to finish her master's degree at the University of Washington—"U-Dub," as it was known. Her doctorate in psychology and subsequent research in human cognitive behavior therapy were earned via scholarship to Pennsylvania. Once done, she couldn't wait to get back west to set up a practice as a clinical psychologist. She wanted to start small and make it her own, and as an only child, she wanted to be near her parents. So a practice in Missoula and the weekly clinical work in Butte, Bozeman, and Billings (the "Highway 90 B-towns," as she jokingly referred to them) were the ideal ways to get started.

Her first official patient came to her when she was twenty-nine years old. Now, five years later, she had already established herself as the go-to psychologist in the area as well as a compassionate therapist. She was serious, dedicated, and very good at what she did.

It was late on a sunny September morning, and Cynthia was just leaving her office to grab some lunch when she was approached on the sidewalk by a tall, handsome man. He looked distracted and somewhat embarrassed.

"Dr. Chan?" Tyler reached out a hand to introduce himself. "I'm Tyler Stevens. I'm a professor at MC, and I was wondering if I could ask you a few questions. Do you have a moment?"

Cynthia looked at him carefully. He was obviously distraught, but there was no ill intent in his voice. "I was just heading over to Dirks for a bite. You can walk me there, and we can chat on the way. That work?"

"Dirks Deli is the best in town," Tyler replied, smiling awkwardly and walking alongside her. He was relieved that she was so easily approachable. He walked in silence, unsure of how to begin.

"So, what can I do for you, Professor Stevens?" Cynthia looked up at him and smiled warmly. His good looks did not go unnoticed.

"I…" Tyler chose his words carefully. "I have a mental health question. To be specific, a question…about the early stages of schizophrenia." There, it was out. His shoulders slumped in relief, but his hands fidgeted, constantly running through his hair and tugging at his collar. It suddenly seemed unusually hot.

Cynthia Chan stopped walking and turned to look at Tyler. Her face became quite serious. "Professor Stevens, if I may…why are you asking this?" She stared into his eyes. She needed to know what she was dealing with.

Tyler smiled slightly. "Sorry…I guess that sounded a bit sudden."

"Look, professor, if you would like to chat about this and perhaps unload some things, it would be best to make an appointment. This is probably not something we can banter about on the way to lunch." Cynthia reached into her purse and pulled out her business card. "I'm happy to meet with you professionally, if you'd like." She put the card into his hand and closed his large fingers over it. "Sooner rather than later is always best," she suggested with a slight grin, then turned and began walking again.

"Wait," Tyler almost yelled. He felt panicky and unmoored, emotions he had rarely felt before. "One more thing." He pulled his cell phone from his pocket and nervously opened up his camera roll and scrolled until he found the picture of him by the fire. "This might help explain things a bit better. Please—can you tell me what you see here?"

Cynthia stopped, looked at him, and then slowly looked down at the phone. She smiled warmly and calmly said, "I don't see anything, Professor Stevens. It's a blank screen." She looked back up at him; she could see the fear in his face. "Why, what do you see?"

Tyler continued to stare down at the picture. It was as clear as day. He felt weak.

"As I said, why don't you make an appointment to see me sometime?" Cynthia Chan suggested, then abruptly turned and quickly walked away.

CHAPTER FOUR

The Missoula College of Montana had six magnificent brick buildings that encircled a large common in the middle of fifty acres on the southern outskirts of the city. Students drawn to it sought a more rural, laid-back setting rather than the busier, more illustrious University of Montana on the other side of the city. The Department of Sociology, where Tyler Stevens taught, was in the largest of the buildings.

September usually found the new students eager to make changes to course selections but not so much with the Sociology Department, and more specifically not with any of Professor Stevens's classes. His lectures were renowned for being original and engaging. There was always a waitlist to get in.

It was Tuesday morning, and the last of the tardy students squeezed into the already packed lecture theater for Professor Stevens's Introduction to Sociology. There were just over a hundred seats, and most were already taken.

"Good morning," Tyler said without looking up from his lectern. He knew it would take every ounce of his resolve to get through the morning. "I would like to start this morning with a quote from Émile Durkheim." On the screen behind him, the quote emerged.

The most barbarous and the most fantastic rites and the strangest myths translate some human need, some aspect of life, either individual or social.

"This was taken from Durkheim's work entitled *The Elementary Forms of the Religious Life*, an assigned chapter of which, of course, you read last night instead of going out with your friends, right?" He looked up and smiled. The room giggled. "Who can tell me what Durkheim means in the context of the chapter you read?"

Tyler was weak and on autopilot. Despite the stress of the past few days, he pressed on. When the lecture was done, he quickly slid out of the side exit and made his way to the staff lounge on the first floor to seek the company of his colleagues.

A handful of professors lingered beside the coffee pot. He was pleased to find his closest friend, Peter "Westy" Westaway, another sociology nerd and outdoor buff, looking up at him as he entered the lounge. "Dude—how was the weekend?" Westy walked toward him and reached out to give him a high five. "Did you get up to that ridge?"

Tyler smiled bravely and nodded. "Yeah, but only spent a night there. Wasn't feeling well."

"Oh man, bummer." Westy looked closely at his friend. Tyler never left the wilderness early. He appeared to be agitated, and he looked pale. "You okay, buddy? You don't look so good."

"Yeah…just a bug, I guess. All good now." Tyler sought to change the subject. "How's Diane?" Diane Branch was Westy's partner of ten years and another of Tyler's closest friends. The pair included Tyler in their lives as much as possible. Perhaps because they felt a little sorry for the bachelor, but mostly it was because Tyler was an amazing guest and friend to them. He was a kind man with an infectious zest for life. On top of it, a superior raconteur who was very popular at dinner parties. "Diane's great; she would love to see you soon. How about supper *chez* Westaways Sunday?"

"Sounds great. I'll bring the wine."

"Okay, usual time." Westy looked at the clock on the wall. "Yikes, I gotta run to my next lecture. Talk later." He slapped Tyler on the back and abruptly left the room.

Tyler grabbed his coffee and also left. He didn't feel like chatting with anyone after all.

CHAPTER FIVE

Tyler Stevens sat at the cluttered desk in his office. The door was closed, and he felt very alone—a foreigner in his own body. He dreaded returning to his empty apartment, and he was hungry and confused. He was losing energy and grappling to comprehend the events of the past few days. He looked at the clock above the picture of him dangling off El Capitan in Yosemite National Park. It was just after 7 p.m., and he knew he had to shake himself into action.

Keep moving, Tyler.

Tyler reached for his backpack and was about to get up when his office phone rang. He slowly picked up the receiver.

"Stevens speaking," he breathed into the phone, slowly sitting back down in his chair.

Silence.

"Hello?"

Click.

Tyler remained seated briefly, then suddenly hurled the phone against the wall, shattering the glass of the El Capitan picture across the room. He then swept his powerful arms across the surface of his desk, causing the various piles of papers and files to fly into the air. Rage, confusion, and fear were simultaneously erupting from deep within his core. He felt desperately scared and alone.

Tyler rubbed his eyes, took a deep breath, and stood up. He threw on his backpack and made his way to the door.

*

Autumn in Missoula descends quickly, like changing the slides of an old projector, and is equally brief. Hunting season enters full assault mode, and the ranchers prepare for a long winter. Nestled in the valley at the convergence of the five mountain ranges that surround the city, Missoula is known as the "Hub of the Five Valleys." This unusually warm September weekend brought most of the residents to the banks of the Clark Fork River for the annual Missoula fair. The college students mingled with the locals, and there was a festive, anticipatory mood throughout the city.

Tyler weaved in and out of the crowd, gradually beginning to relax. Perhaps it was all a dream. He kept moving, as if being preoccupied might help it all fade away. In the distance, he recognized some of his students walking ahead of him. They were licking ice-cream cones and laughing freely. Tyler tried to remember his life prior to his visit to the ridge. Observing his students, with their seemingly carefree lives, he felt a pang of envy. Tyler realized he'd been following them a little too closely and moved back into the crowd.

That evening, Tyler grabbed Thai takeout and headed back to his dark apartment. He was on edge, expecting the unexpected. Exhausted, he headed to bed early. When he eventually awoke, it was already past ten, and the sun was beaming through his bedroom window. He felt a sudden wave of relief through his body. *Perhaps it was a dream after all.*

The rest of the day was spent catching up with marking, going for a long run (a lung-burner, actually—he needed it), and doing the laundry before heading to Westy and Diane's for dinner. He arrived with a bottle of red and flowers. Westy met him at the door and gave him a hug. It was all Tyler could do to hold it together.

"Hi, buddy, great to have you with us." Westy patted him on the back and led him in. His partner, Diane, was just descending the stairs.

"Hi, Tyler," she said warmly. Diane was a salt-of-the-earth kind of person. She hated the trivialities of normal social conventions. She was honest and real, and Tyler loved her for it. She was dressed, as she usually was on most occasions, casually. She wore a loose sweatshirt and faded jeans. She always made Tyler feel at home.

"Hey, darling." Tyler stepped forward and wrapped his arms around her and then kissed her on the cheek. He found it hard to let go. He handed her the flowers. "I know you like lilies."

"Thanks, Tyler. But you don't always have to bring flowers when you come," Diane said, winking at him. "I'll go put these in a vase."

"Dinner is almost ready. I put a chicken on the rotisserie on the barbeque. Been basting it every ten minutes for almost two hours. It'll melt in your mouth," Westy bragged. He was the cook in the family. Like Diane, he cherished close, meaningful friendships, and none was closer than his with Tyler. They had done a great deal of hiking and camping together over the years and had gotten to know each other on a level that neither of them had experienced previously with another male. They were perfectly comfortable in each other's company.

"I can smell it. It'll be amazing, I'm sure," Tyler commented. He was relaxing a little but could still feel the knotted ball in his gut. He needed a glass of wine. "It's Chilean. A Malbec." Tyler handed him the bottle. "Let's get this open and get to it, shall we?"

Westy and Diane's modern kitchen had large floor-to-ceiling, accordion-style glass doors that led onto a sprawling wooden deck. The doors were wide open when Tyler walked in. The 180-degree view of the woods and mountain peaks above them was spectacular. Westy found an opener and took the bottle from Tyler. "Looks like a good one. Thanks for bringing it."

Tyler moved onto the deck and breathed in the warm evening air. He looked up at the mountains. An ominous surge of anxiety shot through his body. It would be a difficult evening to get through; he was so close to Westy and Diane, yet he knew that they would be worried if he opened up about any of it.

"Here ya go, big guy." Diane had walked up behind him and handed him a large glass of wine. "This enough for you?"

"It's a start. Thanks," Tyler replied flatly, forcing a smile.

"Beautiful evening." Diane moved beside him and leaned on the wooden railing. She could tell he seemed a little out of sorts. "How you doing? You seem tired." Diane was a straight shooter; she was as astute as she was intuitive.

"All good," Tyler lied. "Must be the time of year, but I'm not sleeping well. How are you?" he asked quickly, attempting to divert the attention from him. He realized he sounded a little forced and awkward.

Diane looked at him and smiled. She knew better than to pry further. "I'm amazing, obviously!" she replied with a grin. "Life is good here, Tyler. Westy and I are very happy."

Tyler nodded and looked back up toward the mountains. He felt all at once lonely and scared.

"Supper's up," Westy chirped from behind them. He had already taken the large chicken off the rotisserie, and it sat on a platter on the table. "Hey, where's *my* wine, Diane? Do I have to do everything around here?"

"Yup," Diane replied, smiling and moving back into the kitchen. "I'm worth it, remember?" She reached for the bottle and poured her husband a glass.

Westy brought another bottle of wine from the kitchen and plopped it onto the table in front of Tyler. He then took his glass and raised it; the others followed suit. "Cheers, to my two favorite people on earth."

"Cheers," Tyler and Diane responded in unison.

The dinner began with energy and the usual banter and chatter, but soon things became more subdued. Eventually there were longer-than-normal pauses in their conversation. They could tell that Tyler was preoccupied; they instinctively took over the lion's share of the conversation—something they rarely needed to do, as Tyler was usually the life of any party.

Westy knew Tyler well enough to sense his mood. His distance became more apparent as the evening wore on; he appeared anxious and seemed to avoid eye contact altogether when asked a question. Both Diane and Westy knew that when Tyler was ready, he would talk. Tonight, they would push through and provide him a loving place to simply "be."

By night's end, both Diane and Westy knew something was seriously amiss. Tyler was clearly agitated and somber; he had struggled to engage in any significant conversation. Westy walked him outside to his car.

"You seem tired," Westy stated matter-of-factly.

"Dog-tired," Tyler replied. "Hey, thanks again for tonight. I needed it."

"What's going on, Tyler?" Westy looked his buddy in the eyes. "You haven't been yourself since you came back from the mountain when you thought you had a bug. Diane and I are worried."

"It's all good, pal. Thanks for caring. Just need some sleep." Tyler patted Westy on the back, then turned and got into his Jeep, glad the charade was over.

Once home, he slowly got out of his vehicle and decided he could use a quick drink to take the edge off before heading up the stairs to his empty apartment. One block down from his place was The Paw Print, his local. He ordered a pint of the Missoula craft and retreated to the back of the pub, observing the scant crowd. Mindlessly staring at the soccer game on the television in the corner, he was attempting to control the tension in his gut when suddenly his world caved in.

On the television, and in front of everyone in the pub, was Tyler playing his harmonica beside a campfire. It was loud too. Overbearingly loud. Tyler jolted up in his seat, senses on high alert. He was at once both terrified and embarrassed, and he quickly scanned the room to observe everyone's reaction.

There was none.

Tyler leaned forward. The video seemed to be on a short loop. It was playing over and over for all the world to see.

"This Train Is Bound for Glory."

The loop ended the same way each time—Tyler pulling his harmonica away from his mouth and smiling— *right at the fucking camera*. Tyler struggled to comprehend what he was watching.

His mind shot back to that night. He had been so happy. He had been feeling positive and was about to enjoy a weekend in his element. He also had no idea that he was being observed.

Whatever was happening here and now in this pub was beyond his understanding.

Like a cornered cat, he surveyed the room again, ready to bolt should things get crazy. But all remained confusingly normal. He could not understand how everyone could appear so oblivious to the incessant harmonica playing, let alone not recognize the star of the show sitting right here at the back of the pub.

"You need another beer, Tyler?"

"Huh? Hey…Patty…no…no, I'm good, I think," Tyler shouted above the harmonica music. He couldn't take his eyes off the screen. A few people turned around in their chairs to see what the yelling was about.

"*Shhhh*. Hey, I'm right here. No need to shout." The waitress, Patty, smiled and leaned over the table. "You all right, Tyler? You look outta sorts tonight."

Tyler swallowed and tried to ignore the noise. He lowered his voice. "Patty…can I ask you to tell me what you see on that television behind you right now?"

Clearly confused, Patty looked hard at Tyler but decided to play along. She straightened up and turned around to see the TV. She then turned back to Tyler. "Some boring soccer game. Red team against a black team. Why?" Patty leaned forward again. "What do you see?"

When Tyler had eventually drunk enough to get up the nerve to head home, he paid his bill and stumbled through the door. He was beyond exhausted. And for the first time, he acknowledged to himself that he might have serious mental health issues that needed urgent attention.

CHAPTER SIX

When the light from his cell phone came on at 3:37 a.m. and the vibration of an incoming text filled his room, Tyler simply opened his eyes and looked at the ceiling. Though still there, the panic was beginning to be replaced with an "Are you kidding me?" kind of feeling. It was like someone explaining a joke over and over again to someone who just didn't get it. Eventually, you realized they were never going to understand it.

Tyler leaned over and read the text.

This Train Is Bound for Glory.

It was then that he decided what to do next.

*

Tyler knew that determining reality could be a bitch. He also knew that philosophers had struggled with that very concept for eons. What was real or perceived was always a matter of perspective. But his situation was fundamentally more than mere speculation; it was impacting his life. Big time.

Quite simply, he needed to determine if he was hallucinating or experiencing some altered reality. He needed to understand the situation for what it was. For this, Tyler got out a pen and paper and began making notes. He put on his academic hat and decided to take emotion out of it, to merely articulate the facts as he saw them. If anything, he thought, it would provide some ammunition for his shrink.

He decided he would write as objectively as possible, as though he was observing it from above. The first thing he wanted to consider was the medium being used. He thought of Marshall McLuhan's famous phrase—"The medium is the message"—and while he was positive that in his case, the message was more important than the channel through which his messages were being transmitted, it was something to consider. He began writing.

Point one: Whatever or whomever is communicating with me is only doing it, thus far, electronically. Televisions, radios, and my cell phone. There is a favorite time—3:37 a.m.—but it isn't the only time that

I've experienced these episodes. It has the power to somehow manipulate the media.

Point two: Whatever is causing this nightmare seems obsessed with the scenario of me camping. It was the beginning of it all and seems to be the total focus of everything since. The song, "This Train Is Bound for Glory," that I was playing seems important, as does the entire repetitive scene of me by the fire. Everything began and revolved around that moment.

Point three: I am alone in being able to hear and see these hallucinations. The picture I tried to show Dr. Chan and the television experience last night in the pub were nonexistent to others. Undoubtedly this would lead anyone to believe that I am suffering from some kind of delusional paranoia.

Point four: Apparently this is affecting my personality, as everyone seems to have noticed how distraught and anxious I have become. I'm experiencing palpable physical and emotional consequences.

Tyler took a deep breath and continued. The writing was cathartic.

Point five: The most critical point really has no logical explanation. The longer this goes on, I feel that it is more of a communication rather than a hallucination. I know that all people experiencing psychological disorders would probably say the same thing. However, it is what I feel, and it is important to note. Whatever is happening to me feels like it has purpose.

Tyler needed a game plan. In the next column, he wrote down his next moves.

Step one: I need to ask for a leave of absence. I will be of no use to any of my students while I am falling into this abyss. I need time to get well. I will go to my doctor and explain my "emotional exhaustion" and some of my hallucinations (not the full picture just yet) and see if I can get some time off to deal with this—whatever *this* is.

Step two: I need to book a series of appointments with Dr. Chan. It is critical that these begin as soon as possible. I need to know if this is me…or not.

Step three: I need some allies. A support network. Some confidants.

Tyler leaned back and thought, *Most importantly, I need to know if the observer can be observed.*

*

Tyler woke early and felt refreshed. He had, mercifully, slept through the night. He quickly showered, dressed, and made his way to the living room.

"Shit!" Tyler fell back into the hallway, grabbing the walls and attempting to steady himself. "What the fuck?" he screamed.

Slowly, Tyler again moved back toward the living room, surveying the scene in front of him.

It was a giant pile. Appliances and electrical devices from throughout his apartment were meticulously balanced on top of the table in the middle of the living room. The microwave, television, coffee maker, alarm clock, a pair of watches, his computer, and cell phone. And most disturbing of all, despite the devices not being plugged in, the numbers *3:37* flashed in unison on each of them.

*

The next day, Tyler asked Westy and Diane to meet with him on the front steps of the Student Services building on campus; it was time for a chat. The September air was crisp, and the bright sun felt warm on their backs as they walked down to the courtyard and out toward the front gates. There was a small trail that followed the perimeter of campus, and it was an excellent place to walk and talk privately.

"Thanks for coming, guys. I know you're busy. Westy, I know you have a class in an hour."

"No problem, Tyler." Westy put his arm around Tyler's shoulders. Diane locked her arm under Tyler's and rested her head on his shoulder as they walked.

"First of all, I'm not going to die or anything. I'm physically healthy."

Diane squeezed his arm and let out a sigh of relief.

"Thank God," Westy exclaimed. "We thought—"

"I know," Tyler interrupted. "I know you both have been worried."

They walked a little in silence. Tyler was still struggling with how to begin. Finally, he decided just to come out with it.

"I think I'm having some mental health issues." There, he said it. Once released, it began to pour out. "I've been having these weird hallucinations, and I need to figure it all out. It started at Whisper Ridge, and it's continued daily. I went to my doctor yesterday, and he recommended some time off. The college has approved this. He also suggested some treatment to see what might be causing it. I'm going to see someone beginning this week. Her name is Dr. Cynthia Chan. Apparently she's really good at helping people with these kinds of, you know…issues."

Both Diane and Westy squeezed him and continued to walk in silence. It was Diane who spoke first. "My God, Tyler, you must be *so* scared."

Tyler smiled warmly and stopped walking, and he put his arms around them, giving them both a brief hug. Then he stepped back and looked at the two people closest to him. "I have never been so frightened in my life."

*

That night, Tyler poured himself a tall single malt; he knew that sleep would be an absent friend for a while. He sat in silence, observing his apartment like an expectant gunfighter waiting for dawn. While his mood was anticipatory, he felt war weary. Never in all of his many rigorous and death-defying outdoor activities had he ever felt so helpless and utterly spent.

When he finally climbed into bed, Tyler placed his cell phone on the table beside him. He checked the time—

11:23 p.m.—and turned his bedside light off. Immediately, the light in the hallway leading to the living room switched on.

Tyler felt the hairs on his body shoot to attention, and his heart pounded against his rib cage. He leaned over and quickly turned his bedside light on again.

Click. The hallway again went dark.

Tyler slowly inched out of bed and cautiously made his way over to the hallway. His entire body was damp with sweat.

"Hello?" he croaked half-heartedly, poking his head around the corner. The hallway was empty. All was quiet.

He made his way back to bed and pulled the covers up under his chin, again turning his light off. The hallway light immediately snapped on again, and now he could hear the television in the living room turn on and the distinct sounds of his harmonica playing. He fumbled for the light switch and sat up. He was now hyperventilating. "Fuck!" he screamed.

All went quiet. The hallway went dark.

After he had gathered his courage, Tyler again switched his light off and waited.

Silence.

43

When the first gray light of morning finally arrived, Tyler had yet to find sleep, but his mood was aggressive. He quickly dressed and hurried out of his flat, walking to Café Amandine, two blocks from his apartment. It was a 24/7 godsend, and he ordered a large black coffee, waiting for the city to wake and the shops to open.

By 10:30 a.m., he was walking out of the Missoula Electronics Depot with two large boxes. He would spend the rest of the afternoon setting up the cameras around his apartment and syncing them so they would feed into his laptop. By dinnertime, he had tested the playbacks and was satisfied that all was in working order. The most important camera, he felt, should be in his bedroom. He wanted it mounted high enough so that it would record the cell phone on his bedside table as well as him in bed and the door to the hallway. He also wanted a camera in the hall, one in the living area, and finally one in the kitchen. He could now monitor and record all activity in virtually every inch of livable space in his apartment.

Now that the surveillance setup was complete, he felt strangely relieved—content that he was actually moving onto the offense and taking action. He decided to go for a long run. He needed the fresh air.

C.W Johnston

CHAPTER SEVEN

D r. Cynthia Chan's office was on the third floor of The Budapest, a turn-of-the-century brick building on the corner of one of the hippest districts in Missoula. The door to her office was inconspicuous, adorned only with a simple wooden plaque with her name on it. There was nothing boastful or arrogant about the building or the entrance. Most importantly, to Tyler, it felt private.

Dr. Chan greeted him at the door with a warm smile. To his surprise, she was dressed in jeans and a black T-shirt and was holding a large mug of coffee between both hands. Tyler's nerves immediately dissipated.

He quickly surveyed her office. It was really only a room with two wingback chairs, a gas fireplace, and some tasteful modern art. There was no desk, filing cabinet, or any evidence whatsoever that this was the office of a professional. On the whole, it was utterly minimalist.

"I'm glad you came to see me." The genuineness of her approach was disarming, friendly—and completely what he needed.

"I am too," he admitted awkwardly. She pointed to both chairs; it was apparently his choice. He chose the one with the view of the mountains.

"Can I get you coffee? Tea? Beer?" She smiled.

Tyler smiled back. "I'm good, thanks. Nice place," he stated honestly. "I like the vibe."

"Thank you," Cynthia replied. "I want this space to be uncluttered so that there's room to absorb whatever needs to be released," she said matter-of-factly, sitting down opposite him and tucking her legs up beneath her. She was petite but, as Tyler observed, confident, powerful, and attractive.

"So, Professor Stevens, may I call you Tyler?"

"Yes, please."

"Tyler, before we get into the nitty-gritty, why don't you tell me a little about you as a person. Who are you?" Cynthia leaned back and took a sip of her coffee.

The sheer directness of her opening was like a punch, taking the wind out of him. At the same time, he was pleasantly comforted by the fact that he wouldn't be spending hours on meaningless chitchat. He liked the straight-to-the-heart approach. That was how he rolled.

"Who am I?" Tyler paused. "Well, before all this, I suppose I was an easy-going guy. A man passionate about learning and about…living." Tyler looked beyond her through the window toward the Bitterroot Mountains. "Now…" Tyler looked back at Dr. Chan and shrugged. "I'm not sure anymore who I am."

"Tell me about your love of the outdoors."

"What do you mean?"

"You love your time alone. Challenging yourself. Is that pretty accurate?"

Tyler adjusted himself in his seat. She had done her homework. "I like to live out there. Yeah, I love the feeling of being free." Tyler noticed his fingers were nervously tapping the arms of his chair. He consciously forced them to stop. "I thrive on living in this world, not just being a passenger."

"I see. So when you are alone and challenging yourself in these extreme conditions, do you ever feel you are pushing yourself too far?" Chan paused and recalculated her angle. "I mean, do you ever question your own decisions in terms of risk versus reward?"

"I never put the thought of reward ahead of risk assessment," Tyler retorted defensively, trying to remain calm. "I'm in control. I am not a daredevil, if that's what you're implying. I'm always very confident. I ensure the risk is low and manageable."

"I'm not implying anything, Tyler. I'm simply trying to get to know you a bit." She took another sip of her coffee and looked at him, carefully expressionless.

"I love being out there. Hanging from rocks, hiking trails, surfing, whatever. I enjoy the feeling of grabbing life by the balls." Tyler shifted slightly in his chair, wondering briefly if he should have found another turn of phrase. "Is that a bad thing?"

Chan smiled and put her coffee down on the table beside her. She had done some research on Professor Tyler Stevens from Michigan. He was a bright, capable, and carefree man who could have been snapped up by any university in the country, based on his references. However, he seemed not to give a toss about the name of a college or any career ambitions. He was always more concerned about the environment, or more precisely, his ability to access it. He needed to be near nature and to effortlessly disappear into it.

Dr. Chan leaned back. "You prefer being away from people." It was a statement, not a question.

"I love being in nature. I'm not sure I need to be alone."

"So, you could happily be with others…out there?" Dr. Chan kept her eyes locked on Tyler's.

Tyler fidgeted again in his chair. "I think if I was with someone who understood…who felt as I did, then yes." Tyler leaned forward. "I'm not sure what this has to do—"

Dr. Chan pushed. "Why are you sitting in my office, Tyler?"

Tyler sat back. *Fuck, she is direct.*

He took a breath and thought about it for a moment. Then he put his arms in the air and smiled. "Hey, you already know why. Like the pictures on my phone, I fucking see things that aren't fucking there!" Tyler flopped back in his chair and smiled. "So, what do we do now, Doc?"

Cynthia Chan noted the tinge of sarcasm in his question and knew that she was coming off as clinical, and perhaps even cold. She wasn't this way with most patients, but she could sense the complexity of Tyler's character and wanted to cut to the chase. She needed to understand his rationale for living an extreme life and if it was related to the same thing that made him eventually snap.

Cynthia had grown up as the only child in a family full of love. Her relationship with her father, in particular, was what allowed her to become the professional she was. Supportive, empathetic, and gentle, he had provided her with every opportunity to become successful. Nothing would make her want to escape into the wilderness and put herself in dangerous situations. She would never want to jeopardize all the wonderful things that had happened to her in her life. So why would Tyler? What was he looking for...or perhaps running from?

She picked up her coffee again, ever so slowly, as if to diffuse any tension, and smiled. "We do what we need to do."

*

Westy and Diane lived on the outskirts of Missoula. Their home had spectacular cathedral windows in the living room, where one could view the mountains unobstructed. Diane had selected the house. Westy had been in charge of the interior design. Diane always acquiesced because he was so good at it.

Diane was considered by many to be the top ob-gyn in Missoula, and Westy was a popular and hardworking sociology professor. Together they were all heart and passion. They had tried to have kids but were never lucky enough to conceive. Tyler loved them to the core. Since the moment they had all met at a staff orientation at the college, they had connected. It was a relationship he knew would be tested that evening.

Westy met him at the door. Tyler pushed the bottle of red into his chest. "Get this open. We're gonna need it."

By the end of the night, Tyler had told them every detail of his past few weeks. Westy and Diane were silent throughout. Stoic, in fact, Tyler thought. He hadn't left out a goddamn thing. Tyler didn't expect anything, other than trusting that they would be delicate with him once all was divulged.

By the time he had finished, three bottles of wine had been consumed. Westy quietly got up to get some glasses for a nightcap. Diane looked at Tyler and couldn't hide her reaction to her friend's suffering. "Tyler, we will always be here for you. Whatever is happening to you right now, we are at your side." Diane moved over to Tyler and knelt down in front of him. She reached out and took his hands. "We love you. You are family, and we will get through this together."

It was then, for the first time, that Tyler's eyes filled with tears, and he immediately began to cry. Diane reached up and hugged him close, holding his powerful body in her arms as he contorted in uncontrollable, heaving sobs.

CHAPTER EIGHT

Professor Tyler Stevens walked down the steps of his dim lecture hall. It was 9:30 p.m., but he didn't want to go home. He stood behind the podium and looked up into the empty, dark room. This room held many fabulous memories. He adored his relationship with the students he taught, who were all impressionable and eager to learn. An "uncarved block," as the Taoists ruminated. He was going to miss the buzz, the connections, and the feeling that he had a purpose.

Leaning forward on the podium, Tyler pulled out his cell phone from his jeans pocket. In many ways, it was the prime suspect in this investigation, Tyler mused as he opened up his photos. Suddenly he decided to switch on the projector above him with the remote on the podium. Once the projector had paired with his phone through Bluetooth, the massive screen at the front of the hall illuminated the room. Tyler moved around the podium and went to sit in the front row. He looked for the photos from the beginning of that fateful day, selecting the first one and enlarging it. He slowly scrolled through the first few pictures he had taken of the vistas, flowers, and deer trails. He had been looking for that perfect shot.

The pink evening sun had given him some beauties. The mountains in the background looked glorious that day. The pond was like glass, and the reflections off the water made for some terrific pictures.

Tyler slowed down as he scrolled through the pictures of his walk back toward his campsite. He wanted to try to relive all that might have transpired that evening to see if there was any indication as to what was about to unfold.

His pulse quickened as he selected the picture of him. His eyes were closed, and he was focusing on playing his instrument. He was happy. Not a care in the world. Tyler felt queasy; his capacity to understand and handle all this information had reached its limit. Seeing it on the big screen was too much to bear. He was done.

Tyler clicked out of his photos. Immediately his phone buzzed. It was a text.

Fuck.

*

"You feel these experiences are more of a message rather than a series of psychotic episodes."

"Yes."

"And you feel there is purpose to these experiences? Intention?"

"That is what I feel," Tyler replied confidently.

"What makes you feel this way?" Cynthia was determined to keep pushing.

"Whatever it is, it is incessant and glaring. As if it needs to be heard. There is a desperation to it."

"And when you see yourself in this situation and realize what others must think about what you are experiencing, how does this make you feel?"

"Foolish and…embarrassed. Childish. I feel scared."

"Yet you're resolute in the belief that this is something real that's happening. Even when all the conventional evidence may point to some kind of delusion?"

"Yes. I need to explore further. I don't want to simply assume I'm suffering from a mental breakdown. However, I'm open to that possibility. As you allude, logically it ticks a lot of boxes."

Dr. Chan got up to pour another coffee for them both. Her back was still to him when she spoke. "You want to explore further, so tell me, what kind of exploration are you suggesting?" She turned and brought the cups back, placing them on the table between them.

Tyler took a deep breath. "I want a chance to prove to myself that my sanity…my dignity…is salvageable. You know, before I throw in the towel and they collect me in a little truck or whatever they do these days." He forced a grin and picked up his coffee.

Dr. Chan had limited experience with people with "exceptionalities." While she had worked with various clients running the gamut of disorders, never had she met anyone as lucid as Tyler. The objective analysis of his own story intrigued her. He was so confident in his experience, and there was so much clarity to each episode. On top of this, this astute professor was entirely logical in his own deduction of the events as he understood them. The logic of his self-analysis was impressive. She was beginning to think that his illness was beyond what she may be capable of dealing with.

"Let's take this up to twenty-five thousand feet for a minute." Dr. Chan leaned forward. "You believe that the picture of you is appearing on your phone."

Tyler nodded.

"You hold steadfast to the idea that something is attempting to communicate with you through various means, such as, let me see"—Cynthia looked down at her notes— "alarm clocks, text messages, radio, lights, videos, and, oh yes…the television." She looked up at him again. "You also are open to the idea that you might be suffering from a mental breakdown of some kind, but your heart tells you this is not the case. Is that the gist?" Cynthia leaned back in her chair, attempting to digest it all.

Tyler continued to nod silently.

"So what do you suggest as next steps, Tyler?"

Tyler looked up at Chan and smiled sarcastically. "Well, you're the doc, Doc."

Cynthia looked at him intently, then slowly uncrossed her arms. She could see he was scared and confused, but he appeared to be completely honest. Something about him seemed pure and innocent. She was well aware that he had everything going for him. He was obviously attractive, fit, intelligent, and popular; she felt a deep sadness for the pain he was feeling. "Tyler, I'm happy to be involved in this 'discovery' of yours, whatever it is. I will be here if you need me at all times of the day. However, there must be a few rules."

"I'm all ears."

"Each and every time you have an episode, you must contact me. Any hour of the day. I'll give you my cell number. You are to describe in detail what is occurring."

"Agreed."

"Anytime this entire situation becomes overwhelming for you and seems to prohibit you from thinking and acting coherently, you must contact me immediately."

"I will."

"We will meet tomorrow and the day after to get a head start on things."

"Deal."

"We will begin in the morning."

"Sure."

"Finally," Cynthia said as she slowly stood up from her chair and looked down at Tyler, "I need to know that you will be forthright with me at all times. No bullshit. Any crap and I'll terminate our doctor-patient relationship. Is this understood?"

"Makes perfect sense. Thank you, Doc. Thank you so much."

For a long while after Tyler had left her office, Cynthia remained leaning against the door. She felt unglued and uncertain of her feelings. Though she would never admit it, she knew why.

Deep down, she hoped Tyler was telling the truth.

*

Tyler felt a newfound sense of hope, and the tension slowly began to release in his gut. He had warmed up to Dr. Chan. Sure, she was direct and purposeful, but he loved no-bullshit people. More importantly, there was an underlying warmth and empathy about her. He could see it in her eyes. She wanted to be on his side.

Once home, Tyler decided to do some digging himself. He was open to the idea that he was delusional, though he wasn't ready to wave the white flag just yet. He did a search on paranoia and discovered what he already knew: he had many of the signs of schizophrenia. He read that it can fuck up the most basic human attributes, such as speech, perception, what we think, and our own understanding of who we are. A person suffering from schizophrenia will often have a psychotic manifestation, like seeing things that aren't there, hearing voices, or thinking paranoid thoughts...or getting text messages from the boogie man.

To Tyler, it basically sounded like one big LSD trip. He had learned that in the extreme, schizophrenics are delusional in every possible way. It is a chronic mental disorder in which a person loses touch with reality.

Oh goody, my friends, I have a psychosis.

Tyler proceeded to look into the so-called bible of this kind of research: *The Diagnostic and Statistical Manual of Mental Disorders*. From what he could gather, paranoid schizophrenia was the most common type of schizophrenia. *The grand pooh-bah,* Tyler thought. *If you are going to be crazy, you might as well be really fucked up.* Tyler sat back on the couch. He closed his laptop. He had a love-hate relationship with the internet. As a professor, he adhered to the importance of solid scientific research. As a man who was close to losing his fucking mind, he would rather not read any more. And maybe it would all go away.

Tyler tried to recall if there had been any signs. Before that night on Whisper Ridge, were there subtle indications? Lapses in his thinking? Weird occurrences? Sounds? Noises? Anything?

For some reason, he remembered reading about Michael J. Fox's first indication of his Parkinson's disease. It started one morning with a shaky pinky finger. Was it a pinched nerve? One day he's a young man living the dream, and then *boom*, his world blows apart. Tyler wondered if he might have had an early clue. He racked his brain but could not think of anything—*nothing*. The text at 3:37 a.m. on that ridge was the first and only indication that this tornado was going to blow him out of his mind.

*

Before bed, Tyler checked his surveillance system one more time. He almost wanted something to happen.

And it did.

He was only half-asleep when the television in the living room suddenly came on. Full volume. Tyler shot up in bed like someone who was used to the alarm clock waking him for work. He checked his phone; it was ablaze with a text message, and beside it, his digital clock was blinking incessantly.

3:37…3:37…3:37…

Tyler reluctantly stood up and made his way toward the doorway. The hall lights were flashing rapidly, on and off. He struggled to maintain his balance as he moved toward the next room—it was like walking through strobe lights, and he felt dizzy. He could hear the sickening sounds of his harmonica and the coyotes coming from the television, and then, just as quickly as it had started, everything went black.

And silent.

Tyler clutched the wall of the dark hallway. Eventually he felt his way to the middle of the living room. He stood in the center of the room in his boxers, shouting at nothing in particular. "*Fuuuuuuuuck youuuu!*" He sank down to his knees, deflated. Enough. He had had enough.

Tyler began to sob. A little at first, and then a deluge. "What the hell is happening to me?" he called out between the wailing and torrent of tears. He was done, and he knew it. He had reached his threshold. It was all too much.

Professor Tyler Stevens curled up on the living room floor like a young boy desperately needing a hug. He closed his eyes and covered his face with his hands.

The next morning, Tyler pulled himself from the floor and made his way to the kitchen. He needed coffee. It was only then that he thought about his deal with Dr. Chan. Once he had a mug of coffee in his hand, he nervously dialed her number and told her about last night.

"Why didn't you call me? That was the deal."

"I know." Tyler scrambled for words. "I wasn't thinking clearly."

She was quiet. He could sense her disappointment, and he knew he had betrayed her trust. Tyler then remembered the surveillance cameras. He immediately realized he might be vindicated after all. "Dr. Chan, I videoed my apartment last night. I need to check the recordings. Can I call you later?"

He didn't wait for her to reply. He threw his cell phone onto the counter and ran to his laptop on the couch. His heart was throbbing, and his hands were shaking so violently he could hardly type in his password. He opened the security camera program and waited for it to load. He could see himself in real time on camera 5. He nervously clicked on the bedroom camera and rewound it until it read 3:30 a.m. All the camera recordings automatically rewound to that point. He sat down on the couch and nervously let it play.

It was in black and white and a bit grainy, but he could see himself lying in bed. He watched the counter on the bottom of the screen approach 3:35. All was still. It was unbearable waiting, but he wanted to look for any signs. At 3:36, all was still quiet. He had obviously been fast asleep. Then he saw himself bolting upright in bed, his room still dark, but he could just make out his silhouette against the ambient light from the street outside. He saw himself looking toward the hallway and then to the clock on the table beside him.

He watched himself get out of bed and cautiously make his way to the hallway, where he seemed to steady himself as he found his way to the entrance. Tyler switched his view to camera 3 and continued watching himself stumbling through the dark. *Why is it so dark?* he thought, a familiar sinking feeling in his stomach.

Finally, he clicked on camera 4 and watched himself emerge from the hallway. He saw his dark figure move to the middle of the living room, where he suddenly stopped.

Then there he was in the middle of his living room, in the dark, arms raised to the heavens and obviously yelling at the walls. No television, no lights, nothing but a very disturbing image of a madman. Everything was how he remembered it, except the punch line was missing.

So that was it, then. It was time to call Dr. Chan back and let her know that he needed help. A lot of help.

CHAPTER NINE

The first snowflakes dusted the streets of Missoula three weeks after the mountains had turned completely white. It was mid-December, and Old Man Winter was in for the long haul. Dr. Chan had been consumed by Tyler's case. They had met often since their initial formal meeting, both before and after the short Christmas break. He completely intrigued her. He was so ardently convinced of his experiences yet at the same time so completely lucid and objective. She was all at once utterly perplexed and fascinated. She was also fully aware of the dangers of falling into the trap of a charismatic, clever psychopath.

Cynthia had been doing a great deal of research on her own but realized she needed support—or, more precisely, advice. She had cashed in some favors and had in turn been put in touch with a couple of experts, one in New York and the other in Chicago. Through videoconference, she gave them a detailed account of Tyler's story. They listened calmly, and then both were equally candid and insistent that he get professional help. They recommended not waiting too long. In short, he had a very vivid psychosis that could "evolve quickly and without perimeters." In other words, he was unpredictable, and she shouldn't mess around. She also understood that they were implying that he needed someone more qualified than this young small-town girl who knew little about what she was dealing with.

Cynthia got the message, and if she was honest with herself, she knew it to be wise counsel. She just couldn't help but feel an odd empathetic connection to Tyler. It was inexplicable, and she knew she was in dangerous territory. She also knew that she had to level with Tyler. She was playing with fire, and he should probably go to Colorado, California, or even Florida to get the kind of expert attention he needed. She would make some calls. But before that, she had a little more digging to do.

*

It was a Sunday morning in early February when Tyler Stevens walked into his bathroom to weigh himself. He had dropped fifteen pounds in the past few months. Worry had ruined his appetite. He could no longer run more than a few miles, and he was anxious and on edge all day long. The days were spent in a kind of fuzzy daze. The nights were not at all predictable. Some nights all hell would break loose, like a 70s disco, and others—nothing. *Nada. Crickets.*

He never knew what was around the next corner. He could feel himself becoming increasingly paranoid. It was easy to slip quickly into that mindset, and it took all of his energy to stay focused and relatively clearheaded.

He tried to discipline himself as best as possible. Routines were good. Get up, eat a healthy breakfast, and go for a brisk run. Check email, get some groceries, make some journal entries, make note of any anomalies, call Westy and Diane, get some lunch, and so on. It was the routine that helped him; it was also what wore him down. He missed his teaching and, most of all, having a life. Tyler was tired of hiding from himself; he was weak now, and this worried him.

Tyler looked in the mirror. His face was gaunt, and his hair was getting longer—stringy and unkempt. He felt the stubble on his chin and looked deeply into the eyes of the man in the reflection. The person looking back at him appeared lost. A stranger, distant and alien.

Tyler decided he needed to take charge again. He could feel himself spiralling downward, and he needed to take hold and assert himself. *One last hurrah*, he thought as he got into the shower. *Time to clean up, focus.* As the hot water engulfed him, he suddenly realized what he needed to do. It was as clear as day. Why hadn't he thought of it before?

Tyler waited patiently outside of Dr. Chan's office and was giddy with excitement when she finally invited him in. He forgot to take off his jacket; she motioned for it, and he acquiesced. He couldn't wait to chat with her.

Cynthia looked at Tyler with curiosity. He was different today.

"You look good. Refreshed. Haircut?"

"Yes. I feel re-energized."

"What has happened?"

"I've been thinking. I need to try to take control of things a bit. You know, bear down and tackle this thing."

"I see." Cynthia nodded, motioning for him to sit down. She handed him a coffee. She knew he liked it black.

"Thank you." Tyler looked over at Cynthia. "And thank you for being so understanding, Dr. Chan. You never quit on me, and you've never made me feel like I'm crazy."

"Are you?" Chan half smiled and sat back. She knew this would not be an easy session.

"Perhaps. But I need to explore my options a bit further."

"I see." Cynthia reached for her tea. "What options are you thinking of?"

Tyler looked past Cynthia to the mountains. "I need to find out who took that photograph."

Cynthia was quiet at first. She had waited for the right time, and this was it. She decided it was time to confront him, and she took a big breath.

"Tell me about the horrific death of your family."

The look of shock in Tyler's eyes said everything. He was speechless.

Cynthia continued, "Your father was driving. Your mother was in the front beside him, and your older sister was in the back seat. They were returning from your sister's figure skating competition in Detroit. You were at home with your aunt. You were eight years old, Tyler." Cynthia had done her research; she decided to go all in. She knew she had to.

Tyler slowly put his mug of coffee down on the table next to him. He did not look up.

"The police showed up at your aunt's door that night," Cynthia said. "They thought they were speaking to her alone, but you heard the doorbell and were listening from the top of the stairs. They told your aunt that both your parents were killed instantly in a terrible car accident. Broadsided by a drunk teenager in a pickup." Cynthia paused. "Your sister was badly hurt. She was in a coma."

Tyler was frozen. Unresponsive.

"The next day, your aunt took you to the hospital to visit your sister. You went every day for three weeks—you spent the entire day there, holding your sister's hand, crying and hugging her. She passed away two days before Christmas. She was only twelve."

Tyler continued to look down.

"You were young...so very young, Tyler. This must have been unbearable for you. Incomprehensible, even now." There. She had done it. The proverbial elephant was now fully naked in the room. She leaned forward and grabbed Tyler's arm and squeezed it tight. He was rigid.

"Tyler, I—"

Tyler stood up and went to the coatrack and grabbed his jacket. He turned to walk out, then suddenly stopped and looked back at her. He had the look of a man who had been betrayed. He quickly left, scrambling down the stairs to his Jeep. He knew what he needed to do.

With or without Dr. Fucking Chan.

Figment

PART TWO

Figment

CHAPTER TEN

The Missoula weather was typical for February. Snow, wind, and clouds suddenly turning into vivid blue skies and stunning vistas. Today was gray and menacing, but the forecast assured a clear afternoon.

Over the past few weeks, Westy, Diane, and Dr. Chan had tried to reach out to Tyler. He could see their names on the display on his phone, but he didn't pick up. He was in training, and he needed to focus. There were still many episodes, but they were now becoming an inspiration rather than a hindrance.

He'd purchased all the necessary supplies and felt he was fit enough. He looked around his apartment one more time before putting on his backpack and heading down to his Jeep. As soon as he got into the vehicle, he pulled out his cell phone and dialed.

"Westy, it's me."

"Hey, buddy, so good to hear from you We've been so worried. How're you doing?"

"Oh, you know, trying to deal with this—stuff. I think I'm getting back on track."

Westy let out a long breath. "You know we're here for you, Tyler. Day or night."

"I know that. Big hugs to Diane. I'm heading out of town for a while."

"Out of town? Why? Where to?"

"Just away. I'll be in touch when I'm back. Talk to you later." Tyler flicked the phone setting to airplane mode to ensure he couldn't be tracked and tucked it back into his pocket. He started his Jeep. It was time to get to the bottom of things.

*

Once off the highway, he slowed down and concentrated on navigating the logging roads. The first few had been used recently, and the tracks were obvious. By the time he hit the jammer roads, he was more or less following the gaps in the trees above him to stay on the precarious road. His wheels moved easily through the foot-deep snow, and he felt confident that he could push a little further. By the time he hit the final couple of miles, it was getting dicey, and he pulled the Jeep over and parked. He had begun sliding on the ice below the snow and knew that he was pushing his luck.

Tyler slowly got out, pulled on his parka, and fixed his location on the compass dangling from a lanyard around his neck. He reached into the back seat and grabbed his snowshoes, a small modern pair made out of synthetic material, and clipped them on. He put on his thick mitts, shouldered his large pack, and tucked two ski poles under his arm. Leaving his keys in the car, he paused momentarily to get his bearings, then disappeared into the woods beside the barely discernible jammer road.

*

After a couple of rings, Dr. Cynthia Chan heard a frail voice on the other end of the line.

"He—hello?"

"Mrs. Sherwood?"

"Yes. Who is this, please?"

"Mrs. Sherwood, my name is Cynthia. I'm a friend of your nephew, Tyler."

"Oh, how lovely. He is such a wonderful boy."

Cynthia could just imagine this gentle old lady on her phone in Alster Manor in Ann Arbor.

"Is he okay?" There was suddenly a hint of worry in the woman's voice.

"Oh, yes, Mrs. Sherwood. Tyler is fine. He sends his love to you," Cynthia lied. She wasn't altogether sure why she was risking things by calling Tyler's aunt, but she needed a backstory. She had to speak with someone who knew him—*really* knew him—the best. If his psychosis was caused by something in his past, as she suspected it was, then Cynthia felt his aunt might be able to offer some clues.

"Well, please send him my love back. He has turned into such a wonderful young man. He has had such a sad life, you know. But he has done so well. A professor, no less!"

"Yes, Mrs. Sherwood. He is doing very well. Although I can't believe how tragic that time must have been for you both." She thought she might as well go there right away since it had been brought up. It would allow Mrs. Sherwood to assume Cynthia's relationship with Tyler was intimate to the point that such things would be shared.

"Oh my, yes. I don't know how we got through it. I was never able to have children, but I raised Tyler like my own. My husband had just passed the year before, you know. Anyway, I'm so proud of him. Did I tell you he was a professor now? Imagine that."

"Mrs. Sherwood, you must be very proud. You raised an amazing young man." Cynthia treaded carefully. "Mrs. Sherwood, how do you think Tyler was able to get through all of this? I mean, I can't imagine what he had to grapple with."

The phone went silent for a few seconds. "What did you say your name was again?"

"Cynthia. Cynthia Chan."

"Well, Cynthia, I can only tell you that we did a lot of hugging and crying. We did a lot of late-night talking. I took him to church, and we prayed together a great deal. Tyler learned that it wasn't his fault and that he was a good boy with a happy life ahead of him. Now he is a professor at a fancy college out west."

"He certainly is, Mrs. Sherwood." Cynthia pushed on. "So…you felt he was able to grieve and move forward? After the accident?"

"Miss, that boy grieved more than I thought was humanly possible. I imagine, even now, every day he has to relive that god-awful tragedy. It's a miracle he turned out the way he did. I can only thank God."

"Mrs. Sherwood, I'm sure you had a lot to do with it too. Tyler is a wonderful young man." Cynthia knew she had to be careful here, but it was an opportunity to gain a fuller understanding of the extent of Tyler's childhood trauma. She pressed on. "Did you see any change in him after the accident? I mean, did he begin to remove himself from his friends? He must have been so devastated."

"Oh, yes, of course he was devastated. To be honest, it's all a bit of a blur now. I know he spent a lot of time in his room alone. He also liked to go to the woods in a park near our house. He would spend hours in the woods. I guess it was his way of dealing with it all," Mrs. Sherwood said, her voice becoming thin and weak.

"How about at school? Did his academics begin to suffer? Did his teachers notice changes?"

"Gosh, not that I recall. Why do you ask?"

"I only want to find out as much as I can about Tyler so I can help him if he ever wants to talk about it again." It wasn't too far from the truth.

"I suppose people did mention that he'd changed a bit. But he came out of it. He went through a most god-awful experience, but the Lord is good, and Tyler fought his way through it. He was always a strong boy. Strong in body and in spirit, and now he is a professor."

"Yes, he is indeed. Thank you for chatting with me, Mrs. Sherwood. I'll tell Tyler hello from you, though I'm sure you speak on the phone a lot."

"Every Sunday at dinnertime. Tyler calls, and we talk for an hour. It's my favorite time of the week. Imagine him taking the time to do that. He is a very busy professor, you know."

"Thank you, Mrs. Sherwood. Tyler speaks so much about you, I just wanted to say hello."

Cynthia hung up and leaned back on her couch at home. She tried to imagine what it would have been like to lose her parents. Even now she couldn't fathom it. They were her strength and purpose in so many ways. She started to wonder if she had done the right thing with Tyler during their last session. It was still raw; it always would be. He clearly was sensitive, and she had not been. The psychologist in her wanted to see if his episodes were related to the tragedy in his past but, in so doing, she had perhaps lost sight of her humanity. Of his humanity.

Cynthia picked up her cell phone again. He hadn't responded to any of her messages. She decided to keep trying.

CHAPTER ELEVEN

Tyler pushed one arm in front of the other, digging his ski poles into the crusty snow, propelling himself up the slope. The incline seemed steeper in the winter, and he was sucking for air big-time. He was also starting to overheat beneath his heavy clothing. He pulled off his thick mitts, unzipped his parka, and dug into his coat pocket to find a nutrition bar. He was getting closer. It was early afternoon, and he had lots of time.

He took a long drink of water from his water bottle, ensuring he was replenished. He had been in many situations like this and knew he needed to pace himself. He didn't want to get too fatigued, sweaty, or dehydrated. He sat down for a few minutes to catch his breath, calm himself, and refocus. Soon he felt himself cooling down. Above the tree line he could see the clouds parting and a patch of blue sky forming. He closed his eyes briefly to soak in the smell and sound of the forest. Something about winter made everything—every sense—more acute.

An hour later, the terrain flattened out, and he found the deer trail replete with droppings, bits of hair, and some fresh wolf tracks. Tyler followed it until he eventually saw the frozen pond below him and, in front of that, the place where he had set up camp last September. His heart quickened. The place where his world had been turned upside down.

*

Westy and Diane were greeted by Cynthia Chan at the door of her office and were invited in to sit down. They had contacted her a couple of days ago, obviously worried about where Tyler might be. It sounded so strange that he was leaving town with no explanation. He had mentioned Dr. Chan on many occasions, and they thought she might have some answers. She was more than accommodating and seemed almost relieved to hear from them.

"Thank you for seeing us, Dr. Chan. I know it is almost suppertime," Diane said, looking around the sparse office.

"Not at all, please take a seat. I'll grab a stool. And please call me Cynthia." Cynthia smiled. She pushed a small ottoman near the two chairs and invited them to sit down. Diane sat beside Cynthia, but Westy was clearly agitated. He was too wired to sit, so he stood behind the chair, shifting his weight back and forth. Being in a room with a professional who knew and might understand Tyler was somewhat comforting, but it also made it more real.

After some obligatory pleasantries, Westy got right to it. "Cynthia, do you have any idea where he might have gone? He called and said he would be away for a while, but it just isn't like him. We know he's struggling, and we thought you might have some insight."

"No idea. He hasn't returned my calls at all." Cynthia looked at them both. The obvious look of concern on their faces was unnerving, and she felt a pang of guilt. She forced a smile and decided to do a little digging. "You've known Tyler a long time, haven't you?"

"Many years," Westy said. "We met when Diane and I arrived for campus orientation. It was during the summer. He had been out jogging and saw us being shown around. He stopped to welcome us and randomly asked if I played tennis." Westy smiled at the memory. "I told him I did, and we were on the court battling it out that very afternoon."

"Always in action," Cynthia reflected. "I assume Tyler has explained to you what he has been experiencing lately. He's mentioned to me how important you both are to him." She was aware of her professional obligation to confidentiality.

They both nodded. Diane added, "It sounds so very frightening. He did open up to us, explaining everything that was happening. I can't imagine."

"If you don't mind me asking, over the years have you noticed any subtle changes in Tyler?" Cynthia clarified, "I mean, when you reflect on it, can you recall if there were any signs of this impending psychosis? Acting paranoid? Overly anxious? Confused? Anything like that?"

Westy looked at Diane and then shook his head. He moved around the chair and sat down. "Cynthia, there was nothing, and we know him better than anyone. One minute Tyler was a happy-go-lucky, popular member of our campus, and the next he was—for lack of a better phrase—a delusional wreck. It's inexplicable to both of us."

Cynthia thought it equally strange that this had all occurred virtually overnight. Especially with his close connections, somebody would have noticed something. Her mind immediately went back to the ridge and what might have happened there last fall. "I suppose we have to trust that Tyler is cogent enough at this point to handle this on his own. He obviously needs some time to try to get to the bottom of his own thoughts. He's not a missing person because he did reach out to let you know that he would be gone for a while."

Cynthia leaned forward. She decided to come right out with it, aware that she was edging closer to overstepping her bounds as a professional, although what she wanted to discuss was public knowledge. "Has Tyler ever spoken about the tragic death of his family when he was a boy?"

Diane and Westy looked at each other and then slowly nodded. "Yes, after a few years, he must have felt comfortable enough with us to tell us about it," Westy said. "Absolutely horrible. He went through so much. Why do you ask? Do you think it's relevant?"

"Without divulging too much, I think it's kind of strange that he never mentioned it to me in all of our meetings together," Cynthia replied. It was clear she did think it was relevant. "I only found out about it when I contacted your college for some background on Tyler."

"Well, he's quite a private guy," Diane said. "I could see why he wouldn't just come out and talk about it."

"Even when he's receiving messages that no one else is seeing or hearing?" Cynthia asked boldly.

Westy slowly stood up and walked toward the window. The moon was out, and the mountains were clear in the distance. "You believe this tragic event that happened to his family when he was a kid could be triggering hallucinations?"

Cynthia leaned back again. "I'm not making any assumptions, but I think it needs further exploration. I cannot fathom the impact that this kind of event, at such a young age, would have on him. However, I do know that there is no way it cannot influence who he is now." Cynthia looked up at Westy and then back at Diane.

"I appreciate your candor, Cynthia. Everything helps put the pieces of this puzzle together," Diane said, standing up and moving toward Westy.

Cynthia continued, "It may be wise to plan to contact each other immediately if we hear any news from Tyler. And I may need your support when he does return. The next step will be very difficult for Tyler, as he will most likely need referring to a psychiatric physician for tests and possible medication. He may even need to go away for a period of time. Someone as proud as Tyler Stevens may find that a difficult step to take."

Both Diane and Westy promised her that they would comply with whatever was needed. They exchanged cell phone numbers, and Cynthia walked them to the door.

Westy stopped and looked at Cynthia. "Do you think he is crazy, Doc?" he asked.

"I don't know what I think yet. However, all signs are leading to a pretty significant psychological episode. It has consumed him in a short period of time. He is desperate, frightened, and it is altering his life dramatically and completely."

Westy nodded in agreement. Diane stepped forward. "Thanks for meeting with us, Cynthia. Please keep in touch if you hear anything, anything at all. We will do likewise." Diane reached out and squeezed Cynthia's hand, holding it tightly. Cynthia smiled and opened the door for them.

After they had gone, Cynthia walked over to the window. She hated the word *crazy*. People with mental health issues were sick, not crazy. Cynthia looked out at the full moon above the Bitterroot peaks. She had to admit, however, that whatever was happening to Tyler was pretty messed up.

*

Tyler had spent what was left of the afternoon cutting firewood and setting up camp. He had carefully stamped down a level place for his tent, laying pine limbs down as a buffer against the cold and arranging his tent on top of them. He was careful to make sure it was as close to the exact spot as he could remember from his previous visit.

It was now dark, and he had a raging fire going. The warmth felt comforting on his exposed skin. The full moon was now directly above him, allowing him to see around the entire area. Everything seemed exactly as he had remembered, albeit colder and covered in snow. He had eaten the same meal as he did in September and was now leaning back against the exact same log.

It was about 8:00 p.m. Tyler took off his heavy mitts and pulled out his harmonica. It was cold, but he was ready.

CHAPTER TWELVE

Cynthia Chan slowly closed her laptop and leaned back on her couch. She had visited her parents after work and had helped her mom make dinner. Her father was getting weaker, the cancer relentless. He was so strong and determined. In her quieter moments, she admitted to herself that he was going to lose this race, but she would never let him believe that. Her mom's stoic disposition meant she rarely shared her emotions with her only child, something Cynthia put down as a cultural rather than an emotional issue.

They were so proud of her—a professional Asian American woman making a name for herself in America's heartland. She had felt little pressure from them to succeed; they only wanted her to be accepted. And she always was, wherever she went. People liked her and admired her.

From the onset, Cynthia had been a star in the classroom—not because she was necessarily the smartest or because she had the highest marks, but because of her insight and intuition. When other students simply sought answers, she sought a backstory. She was always digging deeper than others. Teachers, professors, and peers alike all admired her fortitude and determination when examining case studies. She was persistent and usually correct in her analysis.

Now, for the first time in her life, she was questioning her ability. She also questioned the disproportionate focus of her workload, and more precisely, her involvement with Tyler's file. His case was now taking up most of her time, and she had cancelled other appointments to do research.

She had to admit that she felt connected to this case—drawn to it on a personal level. Perhaps it was because this case was so challenging that it forced her to push herself beyond her comfort zone, satisfying her professional curiosity. Or perhaps it was because she had initially believed him and hoped Tyler had been telling the truth all along, however bizarre it sounded. There was something so deeply trusting, honest, and passionate about his character that she wanted to believe in him. Cynthia tilted her head back and closed her eyes. Or perhaps it was something she consciously didn't want to admit, that she may have grown fond of him and was concerned on a personal level about his safety. She knew she liked him as a human and felt for his anguish, but Cynthia was also aware that this was where the lines blurred. Nothing positive would ever come from allowing her own personal emotions to enter into the fray.

Cynthia threw her laptop on the couch beside her and poured herself another glass of Chardonnay. She'd had a knot in her stomach since the last time she had seen him. His initial belief in his own sanity had unnerved her; and if, as she suspected, he was currently on a quest to find out the truth, it scared her. She was now feeling lost and without answers. Something to which she was unaccustomed.

CHAPTER THIRTEEN

His hands felt numb from the cold, and his lips could hardly slide along the harmonica. The song was barely recognizable, so Tyler stopped playing and listened to the crackling fire, watching the sparks float up to the stars above him.

Tyler slid the harp into his pocket, put his mitts back on, and leaned toward the heat. It was already past ten, and he decided he should call it a night. Within minutes he had zipped up the tent behind him and had climbed into his down sleeping bag. He kept his mitts and his wool hat on and tucked his cell phone beside him to keep it from freezing. It took over an hour before sleep finally overcame him.

The vibration of his phone against his hip woke him, and he struggled to find it beside him. Tyler pulled off a mitt and grabbed it, lifting it to his face. It was 3:37, and there was a text. This time only three words.

I AM HERE.

Tyler shot up like a startled animal, his senses firing on all cylinders, ready to react at a moment's notice. He listened for anything that might be lurking outside of his tent. He heard only the wind gently whipping at the tarp above him.

He remained motionless, too scared to move. He eventually found the nerve to turn his flashlight on. He watched as shadows danced along the surface of the tent. He strained to listen. He could see his rapid breath in the frigid air. It would seem things had suddenly risen to another level.

He slowly began to calm himself down. It was then that he had an idea, a little annoyed at himself for not thinking of it before. He would reply to the text. With shaking fingers, he managed to type: *Who is this?*

He waited. He could hardly breathe in anticipation. But nothing happened. Tyler waited a few more minutes and then put his phone back down beside him and his mitts back on. He eventually lay back down, pulling his sleeping bag up past his chin, and listened for any sign. He kept the flashlight on and shining toward the roof of his tent. After an hour, he realized nothing would be happening again that night, and as sleep was out of the question, he began to make plans for the morning. He knew what his next move should be.

It was just after eight in the morning when he crawled out of his tent and surveyed the area for tracks or anything out of the ordinary, but there was nothing. He then concentrated on starting a fire. It was numbingly cold, and he needed the heat.

The sky was gray, and snow was a strong possibility. Once the fire was lit, he found the three long poles that he had fashioned into a tripod the day before. He dangled the short length of thin chain he had brought with him from the middle to support his Dutch oven. He gently secured the tripod deep into the snow adjacent to the fire pit and hung the small pot filled with snow from the chain in the middle, gently swinging it back over the fire. He added wood to the fire until it reached the bottom of the pot.

While he waited for the snow to melt and boil, he found a bag of trail mix in his backpack and took a mouthful, staring directly at the stand of alders ahead of him. It was from that location the picture had been taken. After breakfast he would investigate what he felt was his last hope of finding an answer.

*

The local news said the snowstorm would be significant and that driving would be difficult by midafternoon. Cynthia decided to visit her parents on the way to her office to make sure they had everything they needed for the day. Her mom met her at the door and gave her a long hug. The look on her face said everything. It had been a long night with Cynthia's dad, and she was exhausted and worried.

Cynthia walked to the sitting room where her dad was sleeping in a large La-Z-Boy chair, which made him look so small and frail. Cynthia knelt down beside him and took his hand in hers. His eyes opened, and he rolled his head toward her and smiled. In Cantonese, he whispered, "*Húdié.*"

Cynthia put her head on his shoulder and squeezed his hand. "Yes, Papa. Your butterfly is here. How are you feeling today?"

Cynthia glanced up at her mother, who was watching from the hallway and wiping a tear from her cheek. She knew from her mother's anguished gaze that she loved them both so much it hurt.

CHAPTER FOURTEEN

The snow was beginning to fall by the time Tyler had finished his large mug of black coffee. Looking up at the surrounding peaks, he noticed the dark, voluminous clouds descending rapidly, and he realized a significant storm would be arriving soon. He needed to move quickly.

Tyler removed his mitts and pulled out his cell phone. He scrolled through the camera roll until he came to the picture. He then went over to the log he had been leaning on that fateful night and looked down at the exact spot where he'd been sitting. He marked an *X* with his foot in the snow.

He then went to the tent, reached in, and pulled out his large knapsack, roughly dragging it out onto the snow and over to the spot he had just marked by the log. He pulled his hat off of his head and plunked it on top of the pack.

There, now you are me.

Satisfied the large pack would represent the position he was in that night, he looked again at the picture on his phone, wiping away the snowflakes that were landing on the screen. He took a deep breath and began slowly walking backward, carefully at first to avoid the fire, then away from the knapsack toward the grove of alders. The entire time, he remained looking at the picture on the screen, making sure the angle was as accurate as possible.

Eventually Tyler could feel the presence of the tree branches hanging above him. He continued to walk backward until he felt himself bumping into a tree. Without looking up, he shifted a little to the left and took two more steps. He looked down at his phone and then up at his knapsack, now beginning to get covered in snow. Tyler shifted a little more to the left and backed up three more paces. The snow was getting more intense, and he could barely make out the knapsack now. He looked down again.

Bingo.

The photo had been taken right here.

Tyler slowly turned around. The grove before him seemed dense, dark, and unusually quiet. It also seemed to shimmer, like the surface of water. He tucked his phone in his parka pocket and pulled his mitts back onto his numb hands. It was jarringly cold, and the snow was really beginning to come down, even under the cover of the trees. Tyler closed his eyes, took a deep breath, and opened them again.

Then he took a step forward.

CHAPTER FIFTEEN

Two things immediately hit him: light and heat. He felt a little blinded at first by the sheer intensity of the light, and he squinted as things slowly came into focus.

A street. A long street lined with trees and houses on either side. It was hot, and Tyler felt utterly confused and frightened. He turned around to face the direction he had just come from, but all he could see was more of the street. He was completely disoriented. Nonetheless, he took a hesitant step and instantly felt himself falling forward— landing with a soft *thud* onto the cold snow.

Tyler looked up; he could just make out his fire twenty feet away. "What the fuck?" Tyler yelled as he got to his feet. *What the hell just happened?* he thought as he slowly turned around again to face the dense alders. Weak-kneed and breathing rapidly, he reluctantly reached his hand forward, watching it disappear into the thick brush. He pulled it back immediately. "Jesus Christ!" he yelled again. "What the—"

Tyler took a couple of steps backward toward the fire, trying to get some perspective on what was happening and what he had just witnessed. His chest was pounding, and he was dizzy with confusion.

He had seen a street. A long suburban street. It was sunny on that street. Even though it was for a millisecond, Tyler tried to recall what else he had seen. The front yards. There were no lawns. Everything was full of long grass and weeds. The yards were all unkempt, like it was no longer a place where people lived.

What else?

Tyler could only remember the heat and the stillness—it had been deathly quiet. It was summer. It all seemed empty and void of life.

Tyler stepped forward again. He needed to know more.

*

Cynthia Chan's appointments had all cancelled for the day. On the radio, the local news reporter was advising people to stay indoors. Cynthia decided to heed his advice and headed back from her parents' house to her one-bedroom apartment, two blocks from her office. She loved her pad, and, like her office, it was sparse in terms of furniture—minimally decorated, neat, and modern looking.

She sat at the small table in her kitchen and flipped open her laptop, deciding to catch up on some of her notes. Moses, her rescue cat, brought home in a moment of weakness five years ago, purred gently on the chair beside her, pleased he had company today.

Most of Cynthia's patients were suffering from anxiety, depression, or a combination of the two. The majority were fairly young, under forty, which worried Cynthia. Social media addiction was the only explanation she had heard that made any sense. She knew a disproportionate amount of time was spent online. Whether self-imposed or not, people were now under a microscope, one that didn't exist when she was young.

Cynthia looked out at the blanket of snow on her deck. The wind was picking up, and the blizzard was truly beginning. She got up and poured herself another cup of coffee, glad she and Moses were tucked in for the day. As she walked over to the window and took a sip from her mug, she couldn't help wondering where Tyler was and what he was going through. Then she remembered what he had said the last time she saw him.

"I need to find out who took that picture—"

*

This time he was prepared, and he squinted his eyes, looking down as he stepped forward onto the pavement. He could feel the intense heat, and he saw the snow on his boots immediately turn to water, forming tiny beads that rolled off the top and sizzled on the road.

The pavement around him had bits of grass and weeds sticking out of the various cracks that were everywhere; it had obviously been unused for a long time. Slowly Tyler looked up. He was on the same street in the exact location as before. Again, he looked behind him, but he only saw more of the street.

He took off his mitts and placed them on the road beside him—a way of knowing exactly where his exit point was. He resisted the urge to leap back again, despite every fiber of his body telling him to get the hell out of there.

His hands were shaking as he unzipped his parka and slowly removed it, letting it drop beside his mitts. The hot sun was relentless, and he leaned over and pulled off his boots. He pulled his snow pants down and stepped out of them. He was now standing in his long underwear and wearing nothing else but thick socks and a fleecy jacket. His pile of winter clothing lay beside him. He stood motionless, trying to make sense of what he was experiencing.

Tyler did a quick scan of his surroundings, observing the houses on either side of the long street. They had obviously been abandoned—and had been that way for a while. There were some tall trees on most of the properties. The windows and doors on the houses all seemed to be intact, indicating there had been no violence or looting. Where he was exactly was not clear. Obviously, he was still in North America, as the typical cheap suburban architecture was not foreign to him. It could be anywhere on the continent. *But at least I am on* this *continent*, he thought.

There were sidewalks on either side of the road and, further down, he could make out a few cars parked along the street. He tried to look for other clues but could see nothing.

There must be a street sign or something to help me get my bearings.

He took his first step forward on the hot pavement and then stopped to look back at his pile of clothes. As ludicrous as it felt, they marked the entrance of his "portal." *Or whatever the hell it was*, he thought as he looked up at the house beside him, a two-story townhouse with dark brown paint peeling off the sides. He could just make out the address: 24. He would remember this. Now he needed a street name.

Tyler began walking down the middle of the road, slowly at first and then more quickly due to the heat coming from the pavement through his thick woolen socks. All the while he glanced around, hoping to catch any movement or sign of life from one of the houses. All was uncomfortably quiet. Tyler suddenly stopped. There was a white shape directly beside him sticking out of the grass and partly on the sidewalk. He knew immediately what he was looking at. A skull.

A chill ran through Tyler's spine, and he slowly stepped up onto the sidewalk. The skull was part of a clump of white bones. He soon realized it was an entire adult skeleton. It was decomposed to the point of being completely devoid of flesh. It had obviously been out in the elements for a long time.

Someone just left him or her lying out here, Tyler thought, his stomach rolling.

Bits of what used to be clothing lay in tatters on and under the bones. A thick leather belt remained dangling around the pelvis. Tyler shuddered and looked around. It was then that he saw another skeleton about ten feet ahead of him on the side of the road, equally decomposed. Then another clump of bones on the pathway leading up to the house beside him. *What the hell happened here?* he thought as he straightened up again, now noticing what had previously escaped him: other white forms scattered haphazardly along the road. Again, he looked back at his pile of clothes about twenty-five feet behind him, feeling relatively reassured that he still had an escape route.

Tyler looked up at the house to which the pathway led. He decided he might find some answers there. He slowly made his way past what appeared to be the skeleton of a child and toward the front door. His heart was pounding.

The faded green door had a brass knocker smack dab in the middle and a large *28* to the left, just above the doorbell. Even before entering, Tyler noticed the house smelled musty and uninhabited. He reached for the rusty doorknob and turned it. It was unlocked. He slowly pushed the door open.

The sound of the door opening was deafening, shattering the stillness of his surroundings. Once the silence returned, he stepped into the cool, dank hallway of the two-story house. What he noticed first was the picture on the wall to his right. It was a family photograph, one obviously taken in a portrait studio. A young family of four. It featured a tall, dark-haired man standing behind his family. He was dressed in a blue suit and smiling fully. His left hand was on the right shoulder of his petite wife sitting in a chair. She was wearing a white dress with a silver locket dangling from her neck. Her long red hair was tied in a ponytail, and she was beaming with pride. On her knee was a chubby baby boy looking up at her. His older sister sat next to them, dressed in a lacy blue dress, a mouth full of braces, staring at the camera with a giggling grin on her face. Tyler wondered if those were her bones on the pathway outside the door. The thought horrified him.

Just ahead was the living room, and Tyler reluctantly moved forward, noticing the welcoming sensation of the cool tiles beneath his heavy socks. His entire body was shaking.

As the room opened up, he could see more pictures on the mantel of the faux fireplace. He quickly took stock: baby-blue walls, a beige couch and two large chairs, a painting on the wall of some unrecognizable mountain, a coffee table with an empty vase on it. To his left, a stand-up piano, a lamp, and—out of the corner of his eye—a mound of white.

Tyler turned and saw two skeletons lying below the main window. One was obviously the mother; bits of her dress were still visible. Tyler moved closer. He could see her wedding ring on the finger bone of her left hand and, around her neck, what appeared to be the same silver locket necklace from the photograph. Her right arm was stretched out toward the pile of small bones beside her. Tyler held a hand over his mouth as he gagged. He stood up and ran back toward the front door. He needed air.

Who are these people?

Tyler rushed outside to the bright sunshine and once again looked back at his clothes on the pavement. He needed to get some perspective. He ran and grabbed the bundle of clothes, then stepped forward.

Tyler landed face first in the snow, this time without wearing his winter gear. He instantly jolted upright, the freezing wind and snow almost taking his breath away. He looked toward the fire. He could see his knapsack where he had left it, his hat still on top, covered in a dusting of snow.

He hurried over to the still-raging fire and began to fumble his way back into his heavy clothing. He rubbed his hands together over the flames, attempting to warm them. Beside the fire was a small stack of logs. He picked one up and threw it on. He was breathing rapidly, and he could see his breath in the cold air.

Slowly he began to calm down. *What the hell did I just see out there?* He pulled off his mitt and took out his phone. It had mysteriously powered off. He looked back at the stand of alders.

Well, if they thought I was nuts before, they'll have to invent a whole other category for me now.

CHAPTER SIXTEEN

Tyler spent the next two hours multitasking: getting some sustenance and trying to keep warm while attempting to make any sense of what he had witnessed. He moved his knapsack back into the tent after digging out a packet of Mountain House Freeze Dried Diced Beef, his go-to winter camping supper. After filling the Dutch oven with snow, he hung it over the fire and waited for it to boil.

Tyler then pulled out his phone and turned it back on. He plugged it into his spare charger and looked at the time: 4:56 p.m. Enough time for another visit.

*

Diane and Westy spent their snow day making some calls. They wanted to see if anyone had heard from Tyler. Neither his summer climbing buddies, his winter skiing posse, nor any of his hiking friends had heard from him recently. Diane looked out at the snowstorm and suddenly hoped Tyler had hopped on a plane to the Bahamas, a favorite winter getaway of his. She opened her laptop and googled Valentine's Resort on Harbour Island, his favorite diving and spearfishing base. She found the number and read it out to Westy, who dialed it from his cell phone. After a few rings he was able to get through to the front desk.

"Hi, I'm calling because I'm on my way in and my buddy, who I'm staying with, made the booking but is on a different flight. I wanted to know if he's checked in. His name is Tyler Stevens. He's been there many times."

"One moment, sir. I'll check."

Deep down, Westy and Diane knew what the answer would be. Perhaps Tyler had gone to visit his aunt. They didn't want to call her, as she would be very worried if he wasn't there. All they could do was wait until he returned and contacted them.

*

Tyler finished his meal and melted some more snow to make coffee. He sat back against the log, his energy returning. He still could not get his head around what he had experienced today. He had so many questions, and he was dizzy from trying to make sense of it all. Why the hell was he able to walk into a bunch of trees on a mountain and step into summer in the city? Where was that ghostly suburb located? Who were those dead people, and what happened to them? And perhaps most importantly: Who the hell had led him here in the first place?

Tyler remembered the first time he had visited this ridge. He had selected it because, to his knowledge, it had never been explored before. Its name, Whisper Ridge, was apparently a loose translation of an old native name for it. *I wonder what whispers they had heard*, Tyler thought as he poured the boiling water into his metal mug. Leaning back again, he could hardly see the stand of alders through the thick snow and encroaching darkness. He was just about to take a sip when his phone vibrated in his pocket. He quickly put his mug down, pulled off his mitt, and grabbed it.

This Train Is Bound for Glory. I AM HERE.

A shiver exploded across Tyler's neck. He looked over at the alders. All was quiet. Above him, sparks rose rapidly as large snowflakes fell and disappeared just above the flames. The storm was letting up a bit, though nearly five inches had already accumulated on the ground.

He put the phone in his parka pocket, threw another log on the fire, stood up, and made his way back to the alders. He was determined to find out who exactly the "I" in "I AM HERE" was.

CHAPTER SEVENTEEN

Tyler wasted no time in shedding his winter clothes. Leaving them in a pile, he quickly jogged the twenty-five feet to the front door of number 28, the house that he had visited previously. He remembered the man in the picture had looked to be about his size.

Pushing through the front door, he then moved down the hallway, and instead of turning into the living room, he went ahead to the carpeted stairs in front of him. It was dusk now and rather dark in the house, so he began to walk slowly, hesitantly ascending the stairs. The upper hallway was quite dim, but he could make out the openings of three bedrooms and a bathroom. He peered into the first room. It was in disarray; sheets were off the bed, and many of the trophies and toys were on the floor. It seemed to be the room of the older girl. The next room was the bathroom. He could just make out the open vanity and drawers—medicine bottles and containers were scattered across the floor.

Tyler figured that the master bedroom would be the last room on the left. Entering it, he saw that the curtains were closed. He walked over and opened them to allow in the last bit of ambient light. Turning around, he noticed the bed was still made and the room was relatively neat. He found the closet and noisily slid the stiff door open. He scanned the shirts and pulled a short-sleeved one off its hanger; he held it up to his chest briefly, content that it would fit him. He pulled out a pair of running shoes that appeared to be his size. He then moved over to the chest of drawers and felt around until he found socks. In the drawer below he found some jeans folded neatly. As he exited, he grabbed a belt that was hanging on the back of the door just in case the pants were too big. He carefully maneuvered down the dark hallway and stairs, then quickly ran through the tiny entranceway and finally outside.

Tyler passed the child's skeleton on his way back to the road. His stomach surged. He turned and headed toward his snow pants and boots and dropped his booty beside them. He knew he didn't want to spend the night here, so he decided that his summer clothes could wait for him there until the morning. He pulled on his pants and boots, grabbed his parka, and stepped forward.

*

The only other logical thing Westy and Diane had already thought of was that Tyler had gone out to visit his aunt in Michigan; they decided against phoning, as they didn't want to frighten her in case he wasn't there. Westy waited until the roads had been plowed and then drove out to Missoula International Airport to see if he could spot Tyler's Jeep. They knew that when Tyler did visit his aunt in Ann Arbor, he always took the Delta flight that connected through Minneapolis. Westy drove up and down both the short-term and long-term parking lanes; he even got out to examine the many Jeep-shaped cars buried under the snow. Tyler's Jeep was nowhere to be found.

CHAPTER EIGHTEEN

D r. Cynthia Chan sat with her young client. She was a thirteen-year-old who had been the recent victim of a barrage of online bullying and was now suffering from depression.

"Here," Tanya said quietly, handing her cell phone to Dr. Chan, who was sitting across from her.

They had been together for thirty minutes.

"You can scroll down and read it."

Cynthia took the phone from her tiny hands and began to read. It appeared to be a group chat with three other girls. It had started innocently enough but quickly escalated when a girl named Bindy had texted, *We all know Tanya's been seen. Screenshot of her NIFOC! LOL!*

Cynthia felt as though she was reading a foreign language. "I'm sorry—"

"Nude in front of the computer."

"Oh, I see." Cynthia kept reading. A girl called Sally replied, *LMFAO. Yeah, Bindy. I've seen it. Haha. Tanya ur in the shit now! OMFG.*

Cynthia looked up at Tanya, who had started whimpering again. "Is this true, Tanya?"

Tanya slowly nodded. "Now it's everywhere," she said, sniffling and trying unsuccessfully to stop another deluge of tears. Cynthia reached for the box of Kleenex beside her and passed it to Tanya. She moved her chair closer to the teenager and continued reading.

After a few minutes she'd had enough. She was horrified by how nasty the exchange had become once the three girls smelled blood. It was unnerving how quickly Tanya's so-called friends had turned on her. Sacrificing her publicly for their amusement. "What did the school do, honey?" Cynthia asked, handing the phone back.

"Suspended all of us while it's being investigated," Tanya whispered.

"The screenshot they had. How did they get it?"

"My boyfriend—he dared me. Just quickly to show him. You know…" Her voice trailed off.

"I see." Cynthia reached over and rubbed Tanya's arm. The young girl was shaking. "Look, Tanya, we're going to get through this together, okay? I'm here for you. I will not let you down. You'll always have an ally in me. Now, we're going to have a cup of tea together before we continue."

An hour later, as she closed the door behind Tanya, Cynthia thought about her own youth. She had been so focused on her academics and results that she didn't really notice all the drama that happened between the other girls. She now knew well enough how mean and nasty teenagers could be to each other. One thing this job had taught her was that humans have an innate ability to cause great mental anguish to their own species for no apparent reason. She wondered what evolutionary benefit such a trait held.

She checked her cell phone for messages. There was one from her dad. He just wanted to tell her how much he loved her.

CHAPTER NINETEEN

The sun had now burned through the morning fog, and Tyler's fire was roaring. He zipped up his tent and took a long look at the stunning vista below him, then walked toward the alders. He placed his parka and mitts on the snow. Without hesitating, he stepped forward.

It was another hot day, and Tyler immediately removed all of his clothing, feeling somewhat self-conscious standing naked in the middle of the street under the scorching sun. He quickly pulled on the jeans, followed by the socks and shoes, relatively pleased with the way they all fit. Finally, he buttoned up the shirt. He felt more prepared to investigate beyond the few yards he had already seen. Task number one was to find out where in the world he was. Literally.

Tyler slowly began to walk, his senses on high alert. After a few minutes, he picked up his gait and strode confidently down the middle of the street toward the cars ahead of him. He passed more skeletons, all white and covered with bits of clothing but seemingly devoid of decaying flesh. It was then that he realized he had not seen any animals or birds that might have helped expedite the process of decomposition. The quiet was unsettling.

He walked to the first car facing him on his left. He recognized it as a Ford Escape. It was red and very faded and sat down on its rims, the tires long since deflated. Tyler peered into the window of the empty vehicle and moved around to the passenger side. He opened the door and then the glove compartment, pulling out the cover of the owner's manual. It read: *2019 Ford Escape*. Tyler blinked his eyes and read it again. *Last year was 2019*.

He examined the interior of the car. It looked as if it had been abandoned years ago. He tried to make sense of it. His head was spinning.

Tyler found the registration. It was insured under the name Mr. David Sommerville, 34 Langer Road, West Heights, Cuyahoga County, Ohio.

Ohio? Tyler thought. He looked at the last time it had been insured, and his jaw dropped.

January 14, 2020. *That was a month ago.*

"Holy mother of God." Tyler exhaled audibly, looking around the rusted remains of the car. The seats were faded, and it seemed obvious that it had been sitting in the elements for years. "What the hell is going on here?" He now knew that each time he stepped through his little portal—*or whatever the fuck it is*—he somehow ended up fifteen hundred miles to the east and years into the future.

Dr. Chan will have a field day with this, he thought, backing away from the car. He looked further down the street and saw plenty of skeletons on the road and the sidewalks.

Beside him was Mr. Sommerville's house. Number 34. He decided to have a look. The tall oak trees on the front lawn provided some welcome relief from the humid day. If this really was Ohio, it was obviously in the heart of summer.

David Sommerville had lived in a duplex. Number 34 had a metal screen door, which Tyler pulled toward him. The wooden door behind it was already wide open. He stepped through and surveyed the lower floor. Den to the right, kitchen straight ahead, living room to the left. All was relatively neat and orderly. Tyler moved further into the house to the kitchen, where he suddenly stopped. A skull protruded from the doorway at the top of the stairs that led to the basement.

Mr. Sommerville, I presume, Tyler thought, moving closer. Sommerville's skull was darker than the ones outside, but his body was equally decayed. Tyler wondered how long it would take for a body to decay to this point without the aid of animals or the outside elements. Sommerville looked as though he had been coming up the stairs from the basement when he had succumbed. Most of his blue suit still surrounded his skeleton, and a few steps down, Tyler could see his feet were still dangling inside his large black boots.

But most confusing was the military-grade gas mask still clutched within the bones of his right hand.

Tyler stepped around the remains of Mr. Sommerville and slowly descended the dark stairs to the basement. *What were you doing down here?* There was enough light coming from the two small windows to allow him a quick scan of the area. It was a typical basement: a furnace, a washer and dryer, and a few boxes. One particular small box at the foot of the stairs was open. Tyler looked at the writing on the box:

Israeli Gas Mask (Adult) with 40mm Type 80 Filter

(Model 4A1)

RDD USA since 1985

Tyler tried to imagine under what circumstance a man in military clothing would need to run down to the basement of his suburban home and grab a gas mask but not have enough time to put it on his face? He could feel the sweat beginning to form on his brow, and he again felt nauseated.

Tyler climbed the stairs and began to look around the kitchen. There were no photos on the fridge or any evidence of a family. He walked over to the nearby counter, knowing everyone had a junk drawer. The first one he opened by the fridge was indeed that drawer. After a few minutes of flicking through fading bills, payment stubs, receipts, and other random papers, he deduced that Mr. David Sommerville had worked at Cleveland MEPS (US Military Entrance Processing Station). He was indeed single, he supported USAA, and he liked to golf, based on the five golf balls and pack of tees jammed in among the papers.

Tyler opened up the fridge but closed it immediately. What remnants of food remained were covered in mounds of mold. He then turned and walked directly down the hall and out through the front door. He continued walking across the street, looking at the rancher in front of him and heading toward it. He was now on a mission. He needed more clues.

After seven more houses and countless skeletons, there seemed to be no rhyme or reason to the event that had unfolded in West Heights, Ohio, other than one thing— everyone seemed to have had very little warning. The way they had been dressed and the fact that some of the skeletons were in different rooms of the house or in their cars all seemed to indicate that they scarcely had any time to react. They had been walking down the street, playing in the yard, driving a car, or busy with housework when something unpredicted had occurred. They tried, but failed, to run for their lives.

Tyler kept walking down the street, looking at each house as he walked. The addresses were going up: 166, 168 on the left, 167, 169 on his right. Finally, he came to his first intersection, and he looked up at the sign. He was now standing at Langer Road and Fifth Street. He stood in the middle of the two converging streets, turning and looking in all four directions. Nothing but more rows of houses, trees, unwieldy grass, vehicles, and dozens of horrific white skeletons. He walked to the corner and sat down in the tall grass under the shade of a large sycamore tree. He needed some time to think.

He tried to make some kind of logical sense out of everything. The first thing he decided to do was to ignore the portal and his real world. He needed to focus everything on the here and now—on West Heights, Cuyahoga County, Ohio. He had to try to figure out what happened and, perhaps more importantly, why he might have been lured here.

Tyler deduced that this tragedy happened this very year. Or, Tyler corrected himself, in the "Ohio year" 2020. Probably in March, based on the open calendars in two of the houses. It seemed to have happened either in the morning or late afternoon, as lots of cars were still parked on the street and many folks, like Mr. Sommerville, had been at home and not at work.

This event had been sudden, and, by the look of things, it took all forms of life—other than plants. While the beautiful trees were still intact, he had yet to see so much as a bug. Furthermore, it appeared that whatever caused this had been airborne, as not only did Mr. Sommerville attempt to grab a mask, but three other corpses were clutching towels near their faces.

Tyler estimated that the folks of West Heights had around thirty seconds before they had perished, judging by how they were running out to their cars, or up the stairs, or out of their bedrooms. With no prior knowledge of an impending threat, they tried to escape but were literally stopped dead in their tracks. It was an unfathomable cataclysmic event, and Tyler was shaken to the core.

Tyler wondered if it could have been some kind of nuclear fallout. He thought a nuclear winter was supposed to create a dramatic cooling of the climate. Tyler looked up at the sky, and it seemed to be a typical Ohio summer. *And why the hell is it summer here and winter in Missoula?* he thought. *Does time move differently here?*

Tyler looked at the skeletons lying in and next to the street in front of him. They were completely decomposed. If this event happened next month—that is to say, in March 2020—then a fair amount of time had to have passed to account for the decomposition.

So how far into the future am I?

Tyler closed his eyes and took a deep breath. He remembered the last text he had received: *This Train Is Bound for Glory. I AM HERE.* Tyler opened his eyes and looked around the deserted streets, and for the first time, it occurred to him that he may not be the only person alive here in West Heights, Ohio.

*

It was just after 3:00 p.m. when Dr. Chan received a call from Diane Branch. She and Westy had just been phoned by the dean of Humanities at Missoula College of Montana, who in turn had just had a visit from the local sheriff's office. Tyler's Jeep had been found by some snowmobilers on an abandoned logging road about an hour and a half north of Missoula. They wanted to know if anyone knew anything about his whereabouts.

Cynthia then confessed to Diane what Tyler had said to her before he'd left her office. She hadn't regarded it as important because she initially thought he was simply being metaphorical. A quest of self-understanding. She hadn't believed he actually wanted to find out who took that picture. But now both women realized that Tyler had most likely returned to Whisper Ridge.

CHAPTER TWENTY

Okay, here we go, Tyler thought. He decided to continue on Langer Road. Partly because he wanted a straight path back to his portal but also because he felt there must be a reason he kept appearing in the middle of this particular street.

It was even hotter in the afternoon sun, so he hopped up onto the sidewalk to his right. The sun had moved enough to the west that there was some shade from the tall beech and oak trees that lined the street. He quickened his pace.

Tyler made some cursory stops at a few more houses to see if he could gather any more clues, but he learned nothing more. He passed by house 263 to his right, a two-story white house with a van parked in front. There were five skeletons of various sizes, all in a line from the front door of the house leading out to the van, as if they had all been running to the vehicle when they had died.

He continued to make his way south on Langer Road and then suddenly stopped. *What is that?* He held his breath and stood still. He could just make out a faint sound coming from up ahead. He immediately jumped behind the large oak tree beside him and listened intently. His ears had not deceived him; it was a steady, even mechanical sound, like a motor or engine. Tyler's pulse quickened. The sound didn't appear to be getting closer, so Tyler cautiously stepped through the tall grass and crept nearer, crouched like a cat moving toward its prey.

The noise became much louder the closer he got. He carefully moved through the tall grass, ducking behind trees and scanning the area for any movement. Soon the engine noise was deafening. Carefully, Tyler inched forward and recognized its source.

A generator.

*

Cynthia grabbed her coat and ran to the elevator. She had agreed to meet Diane and Westy at the sheriff's office at four o'clock. It was already dark out, so she knew there was little that could be done tonight, but she was anxious for any updates and to contribute where she could. The thought of Tyler alone in the mountains in the middle of a snowstorm made her feel guilty that somehow she had pushed him too far.

*

Tyler was on his hands and knees, moving slowly through the long grass until he was only a few feet from the two-story brown house. The sound of the powerful generator in front of him was overbearing and unnerving. He inched closer until he could make out the large yellow industrial generator, the kind contractors attached to the backs of trucks and hauled to building sites. Two large cables ran from it toward the back of the house.

Moving toward the rear of the generator, he pulled himself around to get a better view of the front door. The ground shook with the intense vibration of the behemoth beside him. Everything in his bones told him to run.

Tyler forced himself to peer around the side, slowly poking his head past the generator and taking in the entire front of the brown house. He could see heavy curtains closed across all the windows, upstairs and downstairs. The black door was shut, and there were no signs of life anywhere. Tyler was about to move closer when what he saw made him freeze.

The address—

CHAPTER TWENTY-ONE

Westy met Cynthia Chan at the door of the sheriff's office and escorted her in. Diane and Westy had only been there a few minutes, but he shared with her what Sheriff Drew Patychuk had told them. The Jeep had been found covered in snow, so it had been in that location for at least two days. The keys were in it, and it was unlocked. There were no signs of tracks or wrongdoing and no evidence of which direction he may have gone. The bottom line was they didn't have a clue where he might be.

Patychuk was a portly man and not prone to humor. He was a by-the-book cop and hated wasting time. He had a nasty feeling that this Stevens character would be consuming his energy pretty soon. He pushed himself backward and up onto the rear two legs of his wooden chair, causing the chair to squeak loudly. He then put his legs on top of his desk, crossing them. The bottom of his worn boots pointed at the three people standing in his office.

"Why don't you tell me your thoughts on what our boy might be up to." He was looking at Diane.

"Tyler's been having some emotional challenges lately. We believe he may have gone to the mountains to seek some answers," she explained awkwardly. Diane realized how weak it sounded.

"I see," Patychuk said, though he didn't. He then picked up his large mug of coffee with the words *I'm a Happy-Go-Lucky Ray of Fucking Sunshine* emblazoned on the front and lifted it to his lips. His chair moaned again as he continued to balance on the thin two legs.

Westy jumped in, attempting to offer some reassuring perspective. "Tyler knows the area well, having climbed and camped in nearly every part of it. Tyler is an avid outdoorsman, and I'm sure wherever he is, he's fully capable of taking care of himself."

"I see," Patychuk repeated, thinking that sounded a bit more promising. He was starting to get a migraine.

After a few more minutes of listening to what they had to say, Sheriff Patychuk decided he was not prepared to treat this as a missing person case just yet. Stevens had let his friends know he was going away, and it was obvious that spending time in the mountains was one of his favorite activities. Patychuk had never heard of Whisper Ridge, but he promised he would look into it. "We'll wait a few more days. Don't get your drawers bent too far out of shape about it until then." With that, Patychuk swung his legs off the side of his desk and sat forward, and with a *clunk* the front legs of his chair met the floor—much to the unconscious relief of everyone in the room. "I'll let you know if I hear anything. I trust you'll do the same." Patychuk lifted his mug back to his face. It was time for them to leave.

*

Tyler recoiled from the generator, crawling back behind the large tree in the neighboring yard. He needed a safe space to reflect on his next course of action. After a few minutes, he decided to take a chance and sprint to the front door of the house directly beside the generator house. It was a small rancher-style home that would allow him to observe without being spotted.

After running up the three steps to the front porch, he quickly opened the screen door and pushed through the large wooden door behind it. The living room was dim. The small picture window on the far wall gave him a clear view of the side of his neighbor's house—a windowless brown wall. Tyler moved toward the back of the small rancher to the kitchen. From the door facing the backyard, he could observe the back of the house next door. He could also see where the cables poked through the weeds and went through an open basement window. Tyler knew they would be connected to the main electrical panel. He opened the kitchen door ever so slightly so he could peek out and improve his angle. From there he could see that all the windows on the back of the house also had their curtains closed. The yard itself had an old bent and rusted swing set and some dead fruit trees, and, like all the yards he had seen, it was covered in tall weeds, brambles, and grass. He looked back at the house and noticed a small porch light was lit above the back door. They indeed had power.

Tyler gently closed the door and moved back to the living room. From the main window he could make out the generator beside the empty driveway. It was still very loud and seemed to vibrate the entire rancher. He found a small chair and slid it over to the window. He sat down and waited, looking for any sign of life.

It was getting late in the day, perhaps around 6:00 p.m., and the sun was well behind the house. Tyler had a choice to make: either he would stay the night, or he would head back to get some supper and some supplies to prepare for a longer stay. He decided on the latter. The thought of a night here with this hellish, incessant noise spooked him.

In under twenty minutes, he had changed and slipped back through the portal. It was time for dinner and a good sleep. He would prepare for his return in the morning.

That night, as he was falling asleep, he thought of the address of the house with the generator.

*

Another night without interruption and Tyler woke with a sense of purpose. The crisp morning air and clear skies lifted his spirits further. After getting a fire going, he cooked breakfast and had a large mug of coffee. He then went to his knapsack and pulled out any food items that would require no cooking—ten packets of beans, some trail mix, a tiny block of cheese, and some crackers. He put all these items in a smaller daypack, then he filled his large water bottle to the rim, screwing the lid on tightly. He found his hunting knife, a flashlight, and his small binoculars and plopped them into the pack.

By eight o'clock, Tyler was through the portal. He was almost at the rancher twenty minutes later, moving into the tall grass and walking under the protection of trees, when he suddenly came to a halt.

The generator had stopped.

Tyler moved closer until he was in the front yard of the rancher and ten feet from the now silent generator. It was eerily still. He waited, wondering how long it had been off. He decided to leave his daypack where he was and to crawl over to the generator. He was low enough that he was still out of sight of the house. Slowly he stood up and felt the engine with his hands—it was stone cold. It had been off awhile, and he thought about moving back into the grass.

Just as he was about to run to the rancher, he suddenly saw the front door of the brown house open. Tyler's heart nearly leapt out of his chest, and he pushed himself down flat onto his stomach while at the same time lifting his head slightly to peer over the tall grass. He could hardly breathe.

It was a man. An older man. He had gray hair and was dressed in brown dress pants and shiny brown shoes. He wore a bright safety vest, the kind worn by men holding road construction signs. Under the vest he wore a short-sleeved dress shirt. On his head, a red bicycle helmet.

The man took a step forward and bent down, wrapping metal clips around the pant legs of both ankles. He looked to his right and then left, and then toward Tyler and the generator. Tyler pressed his head to the ground. When he felt it was safe to look up, he slowly lifted his head. The man had already moved down the front steps and was walking toward the generator. Tyler couldn't breathe. He would definitely be seen if the man came any closer. Then the man abruptly turned at the corner of his house and walked toward the backyard. Tyler tried desperately to calm his rapidly beating heart. He waited, not sure where the man had gone. Then he heard the sound of something squeaking. He raised his head again.

The man was now on a bike, an old upright bike— like the kind you would see in Europe. It was white with a bit of red on the frame. On either side of the rear wheel were two large panniers, both carrying large red jerry cans.

He's going to get gas.

The man moved past the generator to the street, and once there he turned right and slowly pedaled south on Langer Road. The rear wheel of the old bike wobbled slightly and, on each rotation, made a loud squeaking noise. Tyler slowly stood up, watching the man disappear over the slight rise about a block away.

What the hell was that? Tyler thought, turning around and sitting down on the hot driveway, leaning against the generator tire. He was now hyperventilating. The last thing he expected to see was a man on a bike, dressed in safety gear, nonchalantly cycling down some desolate street of a dystopian Cleveland suburb filled with dead people.

Tyler grabbed his pack and ran into the rancher, closing the door quickly behind him. He knew this was his chance.

Once inside, he opened his pack and pulled out his hunting knife and tucked it down the front of his pants. He then found his small flashlight and put it in his back pocket. He was rattled, but he forced himself to remain focused. His years of participation in extreme sports had allowed him to become efficient at controlling his nerves. He had to admit, however, he was currently about as far out of his element as he could be.

Tyler moved across the room and took a quick look out the window. Clear. He went to the front door and, as swiftly and silently as he could, ran across the grass toward the generator, his heart a machine gun in his chest.

Come on, Tyler, you can do this.

He circled to the other side of the yellow generator, crossed the driveway, and ran up to the front steps of the large brown house. He looked again at the address.

337.

He took a deep breath, reached for the doorknob, and slowly pushed the front door open.

CHAPTER TWENTY-TWO

Westy and Diane owned a dark blue Ford F-150 and knew they could easily get near the location of Tyler's Jeep. They wanted to see it for themselves. It was Saturday morning; the sun was shining. Westy threw a small backpack and two pairs of snowshoes onto the back seat. They both climbed into the pickup and headed north out of Missoula.

In just over an hour and using their GPS to navigate the first of two logging roads, they turned one more time and drove east. They could see snowmobile tracks heading down the narrow jammer road as they plowed through the thick snow for a few more minutes until it became too narrow. Westy smiled. Unlike Tyler, they did care about scratching their vehicle. He stopped the truck, and they both got out. Time to snowshoe the rest of the way.

CHAPTER TWENTY-THREE

The first thing Tyler noticed was how dark the house was. No generator meant no power. With all of the thick curtains drawn, it was hard to see anything at all. Tyler pulled out his thin flashlight and switched it on. Unlike the other houses, this one smelled lived in. The furniture seemed dated. It all had a 1980s vibe. *Veritable antiques*, he thought. The entire room felt almost museum-like—caught in a time warp.

He moved the beam of light around the dusty room, looking for any clues. There were no pictures or paintings on any of the walls. There was an old couch, one chair, and a lamp behind it. In front of the chair was a collapsible metal table, the kind used for TV dinners in the 1960s. On the floor beneath it was an old Afghan rug, and scattered a few feet away toward the front window were what appeared to be hundreds of tiny bottles. Moving closer, he could ascertain that they were empty vials—like the kind used for injections—piled high in the corner, haphazardly tossed there after being used.

Tyler pointed his light to the right and saw a small bathroom with the door open. He noticed more vials overflowing from the sink. A top drawer was open, and he saw dozens of packaged needles. *What's going on here?*

He pointed his flashlight toward the kitchen and moved into it, carefully avoiding the various vials scattered everywhere. The dark room had recently been used, as he saw some pots and plates in the drying rack by the sink. More vials were stacked on the kitchen table along with some unused needles. Below the table was a large garbage can. Tyler bent down to peek in. He could make out an empty soup tin, a macaroni box, and dozens of used needles, some with small traces of blood still visible in the cylinders.

Tyler backed out of the kitchen and pointed his light to the staircase. He didn't know how much time he had left, but he wanted to keep looking. He needed to know what he was dealing with.

He moved his flashlight to his left hand and pulled out his hunting knife with his right. The staircase was dark and covered in a worn beige carpet. Tyler stopped after each step, listening for any sign of life above him or any indication of the man returning behind him. There was nothing.

Halfway up, the staircase took a sharp right turn. Tyler followed it and slowly ascended until he stood facing a dark hallway. He shone his light down the length and could make out three doors—the first one on his left appeared to be a bathroom, and he flashed his light inside. Like the one on the main floor, it had a number of vials in the sink and hundreds more in the bathtub. He moved forward.

The bigger room on the right seemed to be the master bedroom. He lifted his left hand high above him and shone the light in before entering. The single queen-sized bed with a green duvet was neatly made. There was a small lamp on the table on one side and a large stereo cabinet on the other. The headboard at the end of the bed and the chest of drawers against the wall to his right were, like the furniture in the living room, made of dark wood and relatively dated. Nothing was hanging on the pale green walls, nor were there any small pictures on the bureau or nightstand.

Tyler went back out to the hall and headed to the next room.

He directed his light on the floor in front of him to ensure he didn't step on any of the vials. There were a few, and he carefully stepped over them and into the last room.

Moving his flashlight beam to the chair beside the bed, he noticed dozens of empty needle packages on the floor. Dangling from the chair were a couple of thick rubber bands, the kind used to wrap around arms when giving injections in hospitals.

Tyler moved the light to the side of the bed. A pair of pink slippers were neatly tucked beneath. He slowly moved the beam toward the top of the bed.

He stopped dead in his tracks.

A body was lying under the faded white sheet in front of him. He moved his light toward the pillow, and, to his horror, he saw a mass of matted brown hair sticking out from under the sheet. He took a deep breath and was about to step forward when suddenly the figure in the bed sat up and turned toward him.

Tyler fell back against the wall, dropping his flashlight and knife, and he scrambled to find his feet beneath him. He rolled to his side and managed to stand, pulling himself through the doorframe into the dark hall. Holding his arms out beside him for balance, he sprinted as fast as he could toward the staircase, not touching a single stair as he leapt down to the first landing, tripping and then tumbling head over heels and finally landing painfully on the living room floor below.

Tyler lay on his back, dazed and in shock. He was breathing rapidly, and as his senses returned, he did a quick mental check of his limbs and joints. All seemed to be in order, and Tyler slowly stood back up in the dark room. He was tempted to keep running, but something about what he had just seen prevented him. It was a girl. She was in a cream nightgown. She had long brown hair and white patches on her eyes.

Tyler stood motionless, trying to catch his breath. His head was pounding. All was quiet upstairs. He decided to find his way back up the stairs to the upper hallway. Without the flashlight, navigating was difficult, but he felt for the walls on either side of him and continued to move forward.

He could just make out the light from his abandoned flashlight shining out into the hall from the last room on the left. He nervously stumbled toward the light and had almost reached her door when he heard the sickening rumbling sound of the generator starting outside.

Daddy's home.

Tyler knew he was trapped. He also knew he needed to gather his flashlight and knife, so he took the last few steps to the room, finding them both on the floor just inside the door. As he grabbed them, he briefly looked up at the bed. The girl with the two round white eye patches was still sitting up, head cocked to one side, listening as if trying to determine his whereabouts.

Tyler hoped he still had enough time to get downstairs before the man returned. He bolted down the hall to the stairs and then immediately slowed down, wondering if the man had already entered the living room. Tyler figured that the opening of the door would have made the generator noise louder. The man was probably still outside. Tyler ran down the stairs to the living room. It was empty.

He turned and headed to the kitchen at the back of the house and saw the door to the basement was open.

The window.

Tyler remembered the cables from the generator entering the open window at the back of the house. He decided this was his safest escape route, and he shone his flashlight down the basement stairs. He was just beginning to step down when he heard the generator noise get louder.

Daddy just came in.

Snapping his light off, Tyler managed to navigate the stairs in the dark, stopping briefly at the bottom to let his eyes adjust to the dim surroundings. There were two small windows in the cold, unfinished basement. The one at the far end was open, and he could see the cables descending to the floor of the basement. Further along, the wires rose up to the electrical panel on the wall.

Then he heard a *click*, and the basement exploded in light. Tyler sprinted toward the window and grabbed the ledge. In one continuous motion he squeezed his body through the window—a move he had made countless times while spelunking. Landing in the tall grass outside, he crawled on his elbows along the side of the house. He could see the red-and-white bike leaning against the wall beside him. The panniers were empty.

Tyler stood up and quickly moved to the corner, peeking around the side of the house. He could see the generator at the front and two sizeable empty jerry cans lying beside it.

All was clear.

After racing back to the neighboring rancher, Tyler quickly opened the kitchen door and dove in. He peered out the window to see if he had been followed. He hadn't.

Tyler rushed to the living room and dropped into the chair by the front window, sweating profusely and gasping for breath. He slowly pushed aside the lace curtains. There was no movement out front either. He had managed to escape undetected.

Unless, of course, the girl with the patches on her eyes told Daddy that she'd had a visitor.

CHAPTER TWENTY-FOUR

It took Westy and Diane about thirty-five minutes to reach Tyler's Jeep. It was still covered in snow. Snowshoeing was relatively easy, as they just followed the snowmobile tracks. Westy took a look at the surroundings and checked the GPS on his phone. Whisper Ridge was straight up from where they were.

It was Diane who spoke first. "Westy?" She turned and looked at him. "I've been thinking. Cynthia said Tyler wanted to find out who took that photograph of him. It was the last thing he said to her."

"That's right."

"Do you think Tyler honestly believes that a person is still up in the mountains? In the middle of winter?"

"I'm not sure what he believes."

Diane looked at the deep snow and thick forest beside the Jeep. "My God, look at that terrain. Do you think he's okay, Westy?"

Westy did not respond. He put his arm around Diane and hugged her close to him.

CHAPTER TWENTY-FIVE

Tyler reckoned it was now late afternoon. He stuffed some trail mix in his mouth and drank deeply from his water bottle, knowing he still had a lot to learn. He needed to know who had lured him to West Heights, Ohio—circa sometime in the future. He felt in his heart of hearts that the girl with the patches on her eyes had something to do with it.

*

Westy and Diane knew they were not nearly prepared enough to ascend the mountain to get to Whisper Ridge. Not only did they lack the equipment, but they also lacked Tyler's experience and ability. It would be foolhardy to even think about it.

Diane unzipped the flap on the pack on Westy's back. She pulled out the envelope and turned to Tyler's Jeep and opened the door. She placed the envelope on the dash above the steering wheel. It was time to head home before dark.

*

Tyler knew he needed to wait until the man left the house again. He was sure his answers lay within 337 Langer Road. Remaining at the window, he watched for any sign of movement. The hours passed, and he was emotionally and physically drained. He went over what he had seen that day and tried to put the pieces together. The needles and vials were obviously significant, as they were scattered throughout the entire house.

The girl with the patches had not made a noise when he had entered her room. She could have screamed or said something, as she was clearly aware of his presence. But she didn't. *Was that on purpose? Is she even capable?*

Tyler thought about how lucky he was that the generator had run out of gas. He would inevitably have been caught had the generator been on the whole time. It was ridiculously loud, and there would be no way of hearing anything else when the man returned home.

Finally, Tyler concluded that he would not head back to his campsite until he had found some answers. He went to explore the bedrooms of the rancher. He would drag a mattress out to the living room and sleep there.

The incessant din and vibration of the massive generator next door made it impossible to sleep. Tyler realized the rancher did not exactly provide the best vantage point. It was very late when he decided to change locations. The moon was full, so a longer, more circuitous route was necessary. He threw the pack over his shoulder, snuck out the rear door, and walked in the opposite direction of the generator house—337.

He must have passed through at least five backyards, all thick with weeds and grass, before he felt it safe enough to cross the street. He sprinted across Langer Road, tucking in behind the duplex ahead of him. Once in the backyard, he headed south again, hopping over fences and avoiding the various pools, hedges, and the occasional animal and human skeletal remains.

The generator was getting louder again, and once he got behind the bungalow directly across the street from 337, he tried the door. It was locked, so he pulled out his hunting knife, pried open the kitchen window, and climbed through.

Though it was dark, the house had many windows, and the brilliant moonlight allowed him to see relatively easily.

Two human skeletons were on the floor below the window, and another smaller one was in the hallway leading to the living room. A towel was still clutched in its hand. Tyler shuddered, cautiously stepping around the one in the hallway, and carefully walked to the large bay window at the front of the house. He could clearly make out the two-story brown house with the black door in front of him. He could tell that the lights were on behind the thick curtains. While the generator was still very loud, it was less intrusive.

And as a vantage point, the bungalow was perfect.

Tyler found a large wingback chair and pushed it over to the window. He would sit here tonight and wait for morning.

*

It was just after dawn when Tyler noticed the black door at the front of the house opening. He shot forward, pulling the binoculars to his face. He focused on the man coming out of the house.

Figment

He was tall and thin. Perhaps in his late sixties. He was cleanly shaven, and his gray hair protruded from his red bike helmet. He was dressed in the same outfit as yesterday. Brown dress pants and brown shoes, and a ridiculous reflective vest pulled over a short-sleeved collared dress shirt. His arms appeared to be bruised. In one of his hands was a black lunch box.

The man abruptly put his lunch box down, leaned over, and clamped his pants with the metal bicycle clips. He looked to his right and then to his left, picked up his lunch box, and then disappeared behind the house. Thirty seconds later, he emerged by the generator on his old bicycle, pedaling down the driveway and turning south on Langer.

Tyler immediately dropped his binoculars, sprang up from his chair, and ran to the back door, flinging it open and jumping into the backyard. He turned right and began running parallel to Langer Road, leaping over the various gardens and debris in his way and pulling himself over several wooden fences that separated the yards. All the while he tried to catch a glimpse of the man between the houses as he ran.

Every so often he could spot him, sitting upright and nonchalantly pedaling his old red-and-white bike. Tyler continued sprinting through the backyards until he could see he was coming to a crossroad. He slowed down and ducked behind a short wooden fence. He could hear the distinctive squeak of the man's rear tire approaching. He had turned left directly in front of him.

Tyler pressed himself against the grass, listening as the squeaking sound passed him. He then poked his head above the fence and watched the man head east. Deciding it would be safe to run on the sidewalk a fair distance behind the man, he stood up and began pursuit. He figured he could easily dive into the tall grass if needed. The man would not be able to turn his head all the way around to see him, and he would have to stop suddenly or make a large turn on his bike to get a glimpse of him following. Even though Tyler's lungs were burning, he felt he could maintain the pace quite comfortably for a while.

Almost a mile later, Tyler began to notice a massive object sticking out from one of the houses on the left. The closer he got, he realized that it was actually much further behind the house, perhaps two hundred yards. He slowed down, trying to determine what he was looking at. His blood went cold. It was the tail section of a massive airliner.

He could see the Delta Air Lines logo. The entire empennage was sticking straight up in the air. Upon crashing, the plane appeared to have taken out most of the city block running parallel to the one Tyler was on now. Bits of the fuselage were still on the roofs of the houses beside him as well as on the road ahead.

Tyler turned and forced himself to focus on the reflective vest gaining distance in front of him. He put his head down and picked up his pace.

What the hell happened?

Fifteen minutes later, the man turned right at a large intersection. Tyler ducked behind a tree until the bike had entirely disappeared, then he dashed to the corner. He glanced up at the street signs: Seventh Street and Marigold. He made a mental note and turned right.

Soon the houses began to give way to more industrial buildings. Tyler passed the remnants of a mechanics shop, an electrical store, and a tire company. In the distance, he could see he was indeed on the outskirts of the suburb, and further, on the horizon, he could just make out a highway.

Ten minutes later, Tyler was beginning to fade. Thankfully, he could see that the man had suddenly stopped pedaling at the top of a hill.

Tyler slowed to a jog and moved over to the tall grass beside him. He watched as the man then glided down a long hill, nearly disappearing from Tyler's sight. Tyler ran forward just in time to see the man begin to brake at the bottom of the hill, turning right through an open gate and into a large parking lot. Beyond the lot was a massive white building that appeared to be some sort of factory. The structure was three stories high, mostly windowless, and perhaps a half a block long. There were a few cars parked in the lot, but like all the other vehicles Tyler had seen, they all sat down on their rims, their tires long since deflated.

Tyler moved alongside the high chain-link fence, noticing the razor wire along the top. He could see that it surrounded the entire compound. Keeping low enough that he wouldn't be spotted, he continued to move down the incline.

The man slowly pedaled his bike right toward another large generator, five feet from the building. He bent over, and Tyler could see him pressing a button. The rumbling sound of the generator filled the air, and a puff of black smoke shot skyward. Two yellow lights on the top blinked on and off. The man dismounted his bike and walked with it toward a large front door, then leaned it up against the building. He pulled off his helmet and rested it on the handlebars. He then removed his black lunch box from one of the panniers, opened the door, and disappeared into the building.

Tyler trotted over to the road and then followed it down the hill toward the main gate at the bottom, the same one through which the man had just gone. He kept as low as he could until he reached the open gate. There was an old guardhouse beside the large sliding gate. Tyler looked up at the simple sign on the fence.

Borden: US Department of Defense, West Heights, Ohio

Tyler decided against investigating the compound further. Instead, he turned and began walking back up the hill. It would take him a while to get back to Langer Road.

I've got some work to do before Daddy comes home.

CHAPTER TWENTY-SIX

He reached the front door of 337 in about twenty minutes. Tyler was unsure how much time he had, so he merely pushed through the door. He was immediately taken aback by two things: how cool it was and the loud music blasting from somewhere upstairs. It sounded like an old recording, with banjos, guitars, and children singing along.

…Hippity hoppity, happy clappy…hippity hoppity, happy clappy…

Tyler stopped and tried to gather his senses. The cold air was coming from an air conditioning unit high on the wall of the living room. And the lights were on. *The benefits of a generator*, Tyler thought as he quickly moved toward the stairs.

The combination of the incessant generator outside and the irritating music coming from above made him feel anxious and vulnerable. He went upstairs. When he reached the hallway, he walked toward the last two bedrooms. It seemed the music was coming from Daddy's room at the end of the hall on the right. It was painfully loud, as if purposefully attempting to drown out the monotonous generator. Some men and children were joyfully singing.

...*Hippity hoppity, happy clappy*...

Tyler poked his head into the master bedroom and tried to locate the source of the music. In the corner he saw the giant speakers, reminiscent of the kind he used to own when he was a teenager.

...*My bunny has come home. Hippity hoppity, happy clappy, my bunny has come home*...

He backed out of the room and, taking a deep breath, moved toward the room across the hall. Her room.

The lights in her room were off, but he could just barely see her under the sheets, thanks to the lights in the hall. The room smelled like a hospice. Tyler stepped closer, the music behind him making his approach unnoticeable.

...*Hippity hoppity, happy clappy*...

Tyler inched closer, trying not to bump into anything in the darkened room.

The music suddenly stopped, and some playful bantering between men and the children began. It was apparently an old live recording featuring silly songs and jokes. A little girl was now telling one.

"Say, Jimi, do you know why the dolphin didn't cross the road?"

"I give up."

"It didn't see the porpoise!"

Audience laughter.

Tyler leaned over the figure in the bed. He could just make out her head on the pillow. He reached above her and grabbed the bottom of the thick window curtain, pulling it toward him and tucking it between the headboard and the wall so that a small sliver of light could enter. It was enough to illuminate the entire room.

This time it was a little boy who was talking above the giggles of the live audience.

"Knock, knock."

"Who's there?" the man answered.

"Panther."

"Panther who?"

"Panth or no panth, I'm going thwimming!"

Screams of laughter.

Her face was pale, and the white patches on her eyes were noticeably soiled and neglected. Her long hair was tangled and unkempt. Tyler guessed that she was about twelve or thirteen. She was gaunt and sickly looking. Her arms were outstretched beside her. They were both red and bruised like those of the man. Tyler looked more closely; both arms were covered in dozens of needle marks.

It was a man speaking now.

"Right back at you, Tommy! Knock, knock."

"Who's there?"

"Annie."

"Annie who?"

"Annie body home? I keep knockin'!"

Everything in his core screamed for him to get out of there. Tyler felt he was risking it by remaining so long, especially being so vulnerable with the racket coming from the next room. However, he needed to try to make a connection with her. He slowly reached out and gently touched her right arm.

The girl immediately bolted upright, pulling her arms away and cowering from his touch. She began turning her head from side to side, trying to get a sense of where the intruder was. Her mouth opened, but nothing came out. She was obviously frightened.

Singing and clapping now.

My dungarees have no knees! Oh my! Oh goodness! Oh me! My dungarees are made of cheese! Well, tickle my ribs and make me sneeze!

Tyler screamed above the audience laughter. "My name is Tyler. Tyler Stevens."

I'm bringing home my baby bumble bee…Won't my mommy be so proud of me?…I'm bringing home my baby bumble bee— OUCH! It stung me!

"Can you hear me?" He touched her leg, and she immediately turned her head toward him, pulling her knees up to her chest. "I'm not going to hurt you," he yelled at the top of his lungs. He was panicking now, unsure of how to proceed.

Then he thought of something. He took a big breath and screamed, *"This train is bound for glory!"*

Suddenly the girl tilted her head to one side, mouth open wide. She leaned forward.

"This train is bound for glory," he yelled again. She raised her hands to her mouth and covered it; then it appeared as if she was beginning to cry.

I had a camel all covered in dirt. He called me squirt, that great big flirt!

More howls of laughter from the audience.

Bingo, Tyler thought. He knew he had just discovered the source of all his troubles.

It was not at all what he had been expecting.

Tyler stood up and did a quick scan of the room, noticing the walker at the end of the bed. He saw hundreds of vials piled up in the far corner of the room. A giant teddy bear sat on a rocker in the other corner. Cognizant that he was pushing the limits of his time there, he walked over to the tall bureau beside the door. On top was a single picture. He guessed it was of the girl when she was a baby. She was sitting in a stroller in front of a swing set in a beautifully manicured yard.

...I had a snake all smothered in cake. It made me shiver and made me shake...

Tyler looked more closely at the items on the top of her bureau. There was a hairbrush, a tube of Polysporin, a small necklace embedded with a tiny pearl. There were bottles of aspirin and Tylenol, an old baby soother, and two pink hair ribbons. Tyler picked up one of the ribbons. *Who are you?* he thought, walking back over to her. He wondered what the hell had happened to her. How had she and her father remained alive when everyone and everything else appeared to be well and truly dead? In his gut, he knew that it was somehow related to the treasure trove of vials scattered around the house.

Tyler tucked the ribbon into the front pocket of his jeans and then leaned over the girl, gently touching her arm again. She flinched but didn't recoil. He moved closer and took one of her frail, cold hands in his, gently squeezing it. Then he abruptly turned and left the room, running down the stairs. He sprinted through the front door, slamming it hard behind him. Tyler continued to race across the street to the bungalow. Once inside, he moved to the window, making sure he had been unobserved. All was still, other than the cursed rumble of the generator.

Sitting down on the chair, Tyler took a long swig of water from his bottle. His entire body was shaking. He closed his eyes, trying to catch his breath and gather his thoughts. He was drenched in sweat and exhausted beyond belief.

CHAPTER TWENTY-SEVEN

He must have fallen asleep in the chair. When he awoke, he guessed it was late afternoon. Tyler sat up and peeked through the musty-smelling lace curtains over to the house across the street. All appeared to be unchanged. He looked up at the girl's window, and that was when he saw the curtain pulled slightly to one side. *Shit*, he thought, remembering how he had tucked it open behind her headboard. He knew the man would definitely notice, as it lit up her entire room.

Tyler thought about what he should do. Going back in would be extremely dangerous. But not fixing the curtain might raise suspicion. The man would surely wonder why the girl would have toyed with the curtains if she couldn't see. He realized he had to risk a quick visit to fix the curtain. He was about to leave when he noticed, out of the corner of his eye, a bright reflective vest. The man was returning on his bike.

Dammit, Tyler thought, sitting back down.

The man rode in front of his house and turned up his driveway. He dismounted beside the generator and walked his bike toward the backyard.

Tyler began to panic.

The man returned to the front of the house, carrying his lunch box, his pants still pinned to his ankles by the bicycle clips. He walked through the black door, and Tyler watched it close. He waited.

About ten minutes had passed when Tyler saw the curtains in the girl's window move slightly and straighten. *Daddy found a problem.*

He watched the house intently, but there was no sign of movement. Tyler reckoned the man was in for the night. *Probably jabbing his daughter full of needles*, he thought, reaching for his backpack. Time for dinner.

*

Tyler kept vigil, waiting until it was fully dark before making his way out of the back door of his bungalow. The moon was still relatively full tonight, so he tucked his flashlight into his back pocket and began to head south. Within ten minutes he had reached the corner of Seventh and Marigold. He turned right and continued jogging. Once he made it to the top of the hill beside the complex, he slowed down, scanning the moonlit compound for any signs of life. The generator was off. All was quiet.

As soon as he reached the gate, he began running across the parking lot. He didn't like being so exposed. A minute later, he was at the large front door of Borden. He pulled the door toward him. It was unlocked.

CHAPTER TWENTY-EIGHT

On the phone, Cynthia's mom had told her that there were some complications. Her dad had been taken to the hospital for observation. She was with him now. Cynthia cancelled her last patient of the day and ran down to her car.

It seemed to take forever to cross Missoula. By the time she had found his room on the second floor, her mom was just coming out. Her hands covered her face, and she was crying.

"Mom?" Cynthia wrapped her arms around her and squeezed her. "Mom, what's happening? Talk to me."

"Dad…it has spread, honey," she managed to get out between sobs.

Cynthia could feel the tears welling up. Her mom continued, "He had trouble breathing, so I called his oncologist. He said to bring him in immediately—" Her mom broke down again and began crying on Cynthia's shoulder. "Oh, honey, I'm so scared."

*

The ominously dark entrance of the Borden complex opened up to a vast foyer and a lone front desk. Tyler swung his flashlight around the room. There was a hallway on either side of the desk. On the wall behind the desk was a faded directory. He walked up to it, pointing his light at the list. It was all sorted according to divisions, laboratories, and departments. He quickly scanned the list, hoping to find some indication of the purpose of this massive building and its significance to the man on the bike.

1st Floor—Communication and Media Relations, Intergovernmental Communication, Business, and Accounting

Department, IT and Technical Support, Security, Sales,
Transportation.

    2nd Floor—Department of Immunology, Center of Influenza
Analysis, Laboratory: Antibiotic Resistance, Analytics: Disease
Control, Analytics: Epidemiology.

    3rd Floor—Laboratory for Bacterium, Protozoa, Prion, and
Fungus, Laboratory: Airborne Pathogens, Laboratory: Foodborne
Pathogens, Laboratory: Waterborne Pathogens, Laboratory: Infectious
Diseases, The Center for Virology.

    Tyler felt a chill, remembering the dozens of
skeletons he had seen throughout the city.

    Realizing it would be foolhardy to check the entire
building with one little flashlight, especially considering the
potential of coming into contact with hazardous materials,
he decided to call it a night and headed back out the door,
past the dormant generator, and out of the compound.

    He would take a chance on following the man to
work in the morning to see what he was up to before
heading back to his winter wonderland and ultimately back
to his apartment. He needed access to the internet to do
some investigating.

    The fresh night air was a welcome reprieve. Halfway
back, he decided he had some time to scope out a bit of the

neighborhood. He turned up one of the roads that ran parallel to Langer—perhaps five blocks away. He was curious to see if 337 housed the only survivors in West Heights.

Fern Drive had a reasonably decent elevation gain, which he felt may give him the opportunity to find a vantage point. Ten minutes later, he determined he was at the apex. A truck had crashed into the front door of the house beside him. He jumped up on its hood and slid into the front hallway of the dark rancher. He pointed his flashlight toward the kitchen. Two minutes later, he grabbed a chair and hauled it back outside.

Tyler put the chair on the hood of the car, then jumped onto it. Using a basic climbing move, Tyler leapt up and grabbed the eaves trough, quickly pulling himself up onto the roof. He carefully moved up to the peak and stood up. From here he could see a few miles in each direction. It was dark everywhere. A ghost town.

Once back on Fern Drive, Tyler encountered what appeared to be an elementary school about half a block away on his left. He decided to take a look inside and trotted over to it.

The front doors were unlocked, suggesting to Tyler that it had most likely been a school day when the event had occurred. He pulled out his flashlight and began walking down the corridor lined with tiny lockers. Dust rose up with each step he took, and soon the entire hallway was murky and difficult to navigate. Tyler pointed his light ahead and, much to his relief, there were only a few skeletons, and those that he did see seemed to all be adult remains. *Either school had not yet started, or the day had already ended*, he thought, slowly moving toward the first classroom.

Tyler turned left through the door. The tiny desks were in groups of four facing each other. The posters on the wall had long since fallen down and lay on the floor. He pointed his light to the front of the classroom and could see the skeletal remains of what he assumed was the teacher. She lay beneath the chalkboard, bits of her yellow flowery dress still hanging from her bones.

Tyler moved closer and directed his flashlight up at the chalkboard, noticing the faint remnants of some writing. He pointed his light to the upper right-hand corner where the teacher had written the date. The meticulous handwriting read: *MARCH 16, 2020.*

Tyler looked over at the bulletin board further to the right. A faded calendar was open to March, and an X was drawn through each of the first fifteen days. *Countdown to the March break*, he thought.

Tyler had seen enough. Once outside, he began jogging, following a side street leading back toward Langer. Time to get some shut-eye; tomorrow would be a big day.

*

Tyler assumed it was roughly the same time of morning when he noticed the bright orange-and-yellow reflective vest emerge from the front door of 337. It was an overcast morning, and it felt hot and muggy, even in his bungalow. Tyler stood up and headed to the back door. They should both be at the Borden compound in twenty minutes.

CHAPTER TWENTY-NINE

Westy called Diane from his car on the way to work. He wanted to talk things through. He had been thinking about Tyler all night long. Westy was trying to deduce two things: first, what was so crucial that a man, knowing he could be suffering from some mental health issues, would leave the support network he had established in Missoula and venture up a mountain in the middle of winter with a goddamn snowstorm in the forecast? Was he that far gone?

Second, and perhaps most importantly, could whatever happened on Whisper Ridge in September to make him even consider returning happen again?

*

Tyler watched the man bend down and turn on the generator outside the large white building. A plume of smoke belched into the air, and the generator rumbled to life. The man then dismounted his bike and walked over to the monstrous white building. Tyler knew this was his chance, and he bolted through the gate toward the generator, hidden from the sightline of the front door. As he reached the generator, he saw the door closing.

Tyler stepped over the bulky cables leading to a small window on the southwest side of the building and moved swiftly over to the corner. He carefully peeked toward the front door, feeling his pulse quickening, a little unsure of his next move. All seemed clear.

He was nervous about opening the door, as he knew the noise of the generator would resound down the halls and the man would immediately be alerted to an intruder. He decided to head back to the small window where the generator cables entered the building. It was open just enough to allow the cables in, and by opening it further, Tyler knew he could quickly sneak through. He glanced into the small, empty electrical room, then carefully lifted up the window, hitched himself up to the ledge, and slipped into the dark room.

The door on the far side was ajar, and the hallway beyond was pitch black. Tyler knew the generator was powerful, but not powerful enough to service the entire building. The man was obviously directing electricity to a limited region of the complex. Tyler moved into the hallway and turned left, walking away from the foyer until he found a staircase halfway down the hall. It appeared to lead up to the second and third floors.

The second-floor hallway was also dark. Tyler looked up the remaining stairs and could see the light coming from above. He carefully continued up to the third floor. The faint drone of the generator was hardly audible now, and Tyler knew each move he made had to be silent.

CHAPTER THIRTY

S heriff Patychuk looked over at the file on his desk and flipped it open. It had been over four days since Professor Stevens had told his friends that he was heading out of town. Based on the snow covering it, his Jeep had evidently been driven to that location a day or so before the storm. There were no signs that he had encountered any problems or that another passenger had been with him.

Patychuk had done a little research on his own and was intrigued by Professor Stevens. He confirmed that Stevens was an avid outdoorsman, fully capable of handling any of the conditions he would face during the storm. He had been involved in many dangerous adventures demanding a high degree of skill. He was revered and well-liked by almost anyone that knew him, so there was no reason to believe he had been a victim of any wrongdoing.

One thing that irked Patychuk, and it was something he seemed to be dealing with more these days, was the selfish assholes willing to push themselves to their physical and emotional limits without having a clue of what exactly those limits were. He found the lot of them to be selfish incompetents.

Goddamned liberals with too much time on their hands, he thought, painfully pulling his ample frame up from behind his desk and moving toward the window. It was snowing hard again. *Serves him right for fucking around with nature.* He put his arms behind him and stretched out his aching back.

Patychuk decided to give it a few more days. Once a week was up, they could begin preparing for a search. A week was a long time for anyone to be camping in the mountains in this weather.

CHAPTER THIRTY-ONE

The entire hallway was lit, though it appeared that only one door, three down on the right, had lights coming from within. Tyler slowly inhaled, filling his lungs and trying to temper the churn in his stomach. With each step toward the door, he briefly paused to listen. A dozen or so skeletons lay in the hallway. Bits of their lives—reading glasses, hair clips, jewelry, and clipboards—all lined the passageway.

When he was less than three feet from the open door, he saw the man's reflective vest hanging from a coatrack just inside. Tyler looked up at the black-and-white sign on the wall.

Laboratory: Airborne Pathogens: Authorized Personnel Only.

His heart rammed against his rib cage like a sledgehammer as he peered in. It was a large room. Recessed into the front wall were a dozen fume hoods, evidently enclosures designed to extract chemicals through their vents.

There were also two big round doors with *Centrifugal Sampler* written on both.

In the middle of the room were six long rows of tables. On top of each one, every few feet, was an aquarium-sized airtight glass container marked *Viral Aerosols*. Each one attached to a small metal tank that connected to the bottom of the table. Tyler also noticed various instruments and beakers lying on top of the tables, and in each aisle between the rows were the skeletal remains of at least ten people, each with shreds of lab coats still attached.

A bank of dormant computers lined the back wall. And on the far wall was another door with a large sign above it:

AEROVIROLOGY. WARNING: DO NOT OPEN WHEN RED LIGHT IS ON.

The door was open. Tyler cautiously moved toward it.

There were actually two thick glass doors, about five feet apart and separated by a narrow hallway. It appeared to be a decontamination area. The inner door was also open, and Tyler moved closer, carefully avoiding the various bones and shattered glass that had been swept to either side, making a path to the door.

The man was sitting at a small desk at the front of the large and otherwise empty chamber. He was facing away from the door. *Thank God*, thought Tyler. On top of the desk was a tiny projector attached to a table. The man's black lunch bucket sat unopened on the floor beside him.

The man sat rigid, arms on the desk in front of him, hands clasped together. He was staring at the large projection on the white wall in front of him. At first, Tyler thought he was watching a movie, but he soon realized it was actually a series of black-and-white maps—slides moving from one to another. The first few images progressed quickly, and then gradually the transitions slowed down. It was on a loop and lasted only a minute or so in total.

The first map seemed to be one of Cuyahoga County. It quickly switched to one representing all of Ohio. A few seconds later, it was a map of the midwestern and most northern states, followed by one of North America.

Each image remained projected onto the wall a little longer than the previous one. The show really began to slow down when the map that included the surrounding oceans appeared. Each subsequent map encompassed larger and larger areas. Eventually, the last slide came up: a world map. Then the entire cycle repeated.

The man was sitting, staring at this endless cycle of images. He seemed emotionless.

Tyler watched as the cycle began its third loop. He squinted his eyes, noticing now something he hadn't seen initially: a shading of light gray expanding rapidly outward from the center of each map until it covered the entire image. Then the slide would change to the next map, and the same thing would happen, only much slower. And at the bottom of each map, he saw a tiny time-lapse counter. He waited until the final map of the world came up again and turned completely gray. The time on the clock read:

7 days, 43 minutes, and 11 seconds.

Tyler slowly backed out of the narrow passageway and into the laboratory. Once inside, he pressed his back against the wall and let out a deep breath. His knees felt weak. Taking one more glance at the scattered bones and broken glass on the floor in front of him, Tyler gingerly made his way across the room to the hallway and, once he felt himself to be out of earshot, began running. In no time he was back on the main level and pushing through the front doors of the lobby, sucking in the fresh air as he ran.

Tyler didn't stop running until he was well beyond the main gate, where he quickly walked over to the tall grass beside the fence, put his hands on his knees, and threw up. Slowly standing up again, catching his breath, Tyler looked back at the vast complex. *What the hell is this place?* he thought, fighting the urge to purge again.

He knew he needed to get back to Langer Road. He still had a couple more things to take care of.

*

Tyler pushed through the front door of 337 without bothering to close it behind him. The music was blaring again. He could tell it was the same record as before, only a different song. Something he imagined one would hear in the 1950s or 1960s. Innocent and naive. A group of men harmonizing with a gaggle of children. The audience clapped and merrily sang along.

…K-K-K-Katy, beautiful Katy, you're the only g-g-g-girl that I adore…

He headed first to the kitchen. Tyler knew he needed a name. He began opening drawers, looking for anything that would give him a clue, trying to keep his nerves in check. His entire body was screaming to get back to his portal, away from this nightmare. He didn't know how much time he had.

In the first drawer, he found some cutlery. In all the others, a stash of needles, syringes, and boxes stuffed with vials. *Go figure*, he thought. He picked up one of the boxes and read the sticker on the side: *TANGER MMR P6 Antigen/Biomolecular XX70. For research only. Not for human consumption. Borden.*

Tyler moved back to the living room. In the corner was a tiny table with a drawer near the top. Tyler went over and rifled through old sheets of paper, pencils, and two syringes. There were more needles and underneath…an envelope. *Jackpot*, he thought. It was an unopened letter from the Cuyahoga County Probate Court Marriage License Department. Tyler held it up to get a better look. The year stamped on the front was 2013.

He glanced below the stamp and saw the address:

Dr. Elias LARSSON and Mrs. Angel LARSSON

337 Langer Rd

West Heights, Cuyahoga County

Ohio

44192

Tyler placed the envelope back in the drawer and closed it. He found it strange that a woman had ever lived here, as the whole place felt devoid of feeling. Cold. A house, not a home.

Tyler turned and headed toward the stairs. The music in the upper hallway was overbearing.

…Turn around and jump down and pick up the bunny, turn around and jump down and get back up!…Turn around and jump down and pick up the bunny. Hug him and tickle him and don't give up!…

Tyler ran down the corridor to the room on the left. It was still completely dark. He reached up to the wall beside him and flicked on the light switch. For the first time, he could see the entire room clearly. The girl was lying under a stained white sheet. Her eye patches were taped to her face. She was unaware of his presence.

The song ended. Tyler could hear the audience clapping. The guitars and banjo started again.

…Bark, bark, bark goes the doggie…Everybody sing along!…Bark, bark, bark goes the doggie…

Tyler reached out and gently touched the girl's right shin. She immediately sat up and turned her head in his direction. She started trembling. Her mouth opened, and

Tyler could see, beyond her horribly chapped lips, that her teeth were rotten and her mouth was full of sores. He looked down at her arms. They were terribly swollen and bruised. Purple and red lesions seemed to be everywhere on her body. *What in God's name happened to you?* he thought, reaching forward and taking her cold right hand in his. She did not resist.

...Bark-ity-bark...bark-ity-bark...bark-ity-bark goes the puppy too...

Tyler leaned closer to the girl and bellowed, "This train is bound for glory!"

The girl closed her mouth and cocked her head toward him. Ever so slowly, a tiny smile swept across her face. Tyler squeezed her hand and let go. It was time to go home.

Tyler bolted out of the room, down the stairs, and out the front door. He continued to run across the street to the bungalow so he could pick up his daypack and finish off the remaining water—he was parched. When he was done, he stuffed the empty bottle, his knife, and the flashlight into it. He would leave his remaining food behind.

Tyler suddenly remembered the pink ribbon he had taken from the top of the girl's bureau. He pulled the ribbon out of his front pocket and threw it into the pack along with the other items. He then slung the pack over his shoulder and ran to the front door.

He immediately stopped.

Standing in the front yard facing the bungalow was a man in a bright reflective vest with bicycle clips around his ankles. He was wearing a red bike helmet and, much to Tyler's horror, was pointing a very large weapon directly at his chest.

Daddy doesn't look happy.

Figment

PART THREE

Figment

CHAPTER THIRTY-TWO

The room was obviously a basement. It was filled with dozens of boxes. Tyler could just make out the Borden logo on each one. Like him, the boxes appeared to be upside down.

He pushed his chin to his chest. The thick chains holding his legs up to the ceiling beam were killing him. His hands were also secured behind his back with what felt like plastic zip ties. He had a sharp pain in his shoulder.

He wasn't sure how long he had been hanging there, but he had only just regained consciousness. Tyler turned his head and saw an open window with cables snaking through. It was getting dark outside. He could see his daypack on the floor below the window.

Tyler looked toward the stairs. The basement lights were off, but a light was coming from the kitchen door above. He could hear the incessant generator outside and the miserably happy sounds of children singing above him.

Tyler began to get dizzy again, and slowly the world faded to black.

*

When he awoke, his head was pounding, and the light was on.

And this time he was not alone.

Tyler could see a pair of shiny brown shoes sticking out from beneath dark dress pants. The man was standing just a few feet away. Tyler felt himself dropping, and soon his forehead roughly bumped against the hard floor. Seconds later, he was lying belly-down on the mercifully cold concrete. His arms were bound tightly behind him. Every part of his body throbbed with pain, but the floor was a welcome relief.

Tyler turned his eyes upward. His vision was blurred, but he could see the man holding a rope. It was connected to a rustic pulley system. The crank for the pulley was rigged onto a metal pole in the middle of the room, perhaps six feet away. Tyler quickly turned his head the other way, desperately trying to figure out his options. There weren't any.

Tyler slowly turned his head back around. The man's brown shoes were now only inches from his face. A hand moved toward him, and a white patch descended over his right eye. He felt the tape being pressed roughly against his eyebrow and cheek. The man immediately did the same with his other eye. All went dark.

Tyler waited in fear, trying to hear what was happening around him. His senses were on overload, and he felt like vomiting. He could just make out the sound of the pulley, the rattle of chains, and then his own agonizing scream.

The excruciating pain shot through his entire body like a streak of electricity. He was being quickly hoisted back toward the ceiling. Tyler screamed again, sensing himself now swinging in the air. He was paralyzed with terror. The image of a carcass dangling from a metal hook at some slaughterhouse was the last thing he thought of before blacking out.

*

Tyler woke to find himself sitting on the concrete floor, leaning up against a pole. He assumed it was the same pole with the crank for the pulley. His head was throbbing, and he was beyond thirsty.

His arms were still secured behind him, though this time he could feel they were wrapped around the pole itself. He could also feel that his legs were free of the cursed chains. He painfully drew his knees up toward his chest. He tried to speak, but his throat was too dry.

Tyler could see nothing. The patches were tight and effective. The music and the generator were on full throttle, so he had no idea if he was alone. He also had no sense of how long he had been in this chamber of horrors.

Suddenly he heard the generator shutting down. He listened as it grumbled and sputtered and eventually went completely silent. The music stopped. The quiet was unnerving, and Tyler strained to listen for any sound.

After a few seconds, he heard the front door close, followed by a *clunk, clunk, clunk* of footsteps heading toward the kitchen. He could only assume it was his captor slowly descending the stairs and walking toward him.

Tyler pressed his back against the cold pole, his entire body rigid and anticipatory. Suddenly he felt both eye patches being simultaneously ripped off his face. The intense light made him squeeze his eyes shut. Slowly Tyler began to open them as the light seemed to move away from his face. The man was about two feet in front of him, sitting on a small wooden stool. His wild gray hair shot up in every direction. His eyes were wide and angry.

The man was holding what looked like a small machete in his right hand, and a large flashlight sat on the ground in front of him, now pointing at Tyler's ankles. He was staring at him with contempt.

Tyler again tried to speak, but nothing emerged from his dry throat.

"You have a lot of explaining to do." The man's voice was weak and high-pitched. Not at all what Tyler was expecting. It was the kind of voice that hadn't been used for a long time. His entire demeanor was a mixture of curiosity and disdain. Tyler could only look back at him in absolute panic.

"Where did you come from?" the man squeaked, tipping his head to one shoulder and shrugging.

Again, Tyler tried to speak. He closed his lips, attempting to swallow, but there was no moisture in his throat.

The man shifted in his chair. He seemed agitated. "You're going to tell me, or I will disembowel you," the man croaked matter-of-factly, staring directly into Tyler's eyes and waving the machete in front of the flashlight.

What the fuck. Tyler was paralyzed with terror. He could hardly breathe.

"Don't think I won't do it. I did it to my wife, you know. She deserved it, though. She was a bitch and needed to die," he stated coldly, leaning closer to Tyler. Tyler could smell his foul breath and see the lesions on his skin. "You were in my daughter's room." It was a statement. "You shouldn't have gone there."

Tyler was fading. He found it hard to follow the man's train of thought. He simply nodded, agreeing with him. It was all he could do.

"I will kill you, you know," the man mused, sitting back and observing his captive, indicating it was a fait accompli.

Tyler did not move. He was staring into the eyes of a man who was clearly deranged. He glanced down at his own legs, tucked up to his chest. He could see the blood on his jeans near his ankles where the chains had been. He looked back up at the man and mouthed, "Water," hoping he could buy himself some time. Perhaps curiosity would prevent Dr. Elias Larsson from killing him. At least until he heard what he had to say.

The man tipped his head to one side and studied Tyler as if considering his options. He brought the flashlight up and shone it directly at his face. Tyler closed his eyes and turned his head away.

"I will kill you slowly, though. You shouldn't have gone to my daughter's room. She is unwell. What is your name?" The man fired off questions in rapid succession. "I kill everything, you know. It's what I do. Not my daughter, though. She is special. You shouldn't have gone to her fucking room." The man was screaming now. "Why did you follow me to work? I do important work, you know. Why were you there? I knew you were, you know. Did you enjoy the show?"

Tyler couldn't move. *I'm going to die in this basement.*

The light suddenly moved away from his face, and Tyler reluctantly turned his head back toward the man. He was now hovering directly over him. "I shot you with a tranquilizer. Hit you right in the fucking shoulder, then strung you up like a deer from the fucking beam," he squeaked, gradually breaking into a grin. "I'm good with chemicals, you know. I'm going to give you some now."

Figment

Tyler felt the sharp jab of a needle in his arm. Everything began to go hazy. He could hear the man moving the chains toward him when everything went black.

CHAPTER THIRTY-THREE

I t was wet. He was drowning. Tyler lifted his head and gasped for air. He couldn't see, but he could feel the cold steel bowl of water beneath his chin. He was on his stomach, lying on the concrete floor. He was naked.

His arms were still tied behind him, and Tyler could feel the tight chains around his raw ankles. He had no idea how long he had been unconscious. He could hear the generator at the front of the house and the music above him. He felt like dying.

He moved his head slowly back down toward the bowl and felt the water on his lips. He stuck his tongue out. The water was cold, and he lowered his entire mouth to the surface and, with great difficulty, began to sip, forcing it down his burning throat. He knew that Daddy was buttering him up to get some information.

He drank the bowl dry, licking the final few drops from the bottom. As he lifted his head again, he heard the bowl being kicked to one side.

"You want to meet my wife?"

Tyler froze. He then felt the man grab his arms behind him and pull him backward—the pain was unbearable, and he screamed out in anguish.

"Sit up," the man hollered above the din.

Tyler slowly rolled to his side and tried to sit up, but he was too weak.

"Sit the fuck up, or I'll cut your balls off."

Tyler cringed and tried again, attempting to roll to his knees, but his ankles were still bound. He fell back down.

Out of sheer fear, he gave it one more attempt, and this time he managed to make it up to his knees. He sat on his heels and waited. He was beginning to shiver uncontrollably. His eye patches prevented him from seeing anything.

"I said, do you want to meet my wife?"

Tyler didn't know if he should nod or shake his head. Did he mean meet her in the "You will be dead too" sense? Or did he mean literally meet her? Tyler didn't move.

He suddenly felt the eye patches being ripped from his face, and he squinted from the blinding light. Slowly his vision returned, and the man was moving toward the stool, about four feet from him. He sat down to face Tyler. The lights in the basement were very bright, and many boxes were piled up behind the man. Tyler cleared his throat and tried to speak. "I—I don't understand," he whispered.

"What did you say?" the man yelled angrily above the noise of the generator. He had a crazed look in his eyes.

Tyler tried again, this time slightly louder. "I don't understand."

The man was enraged. He suddenly got up and stepped toward Tyler, drawing his arm up behind him and slapping him hard across the face, almost knocking him over again. "You should meet her," he screamed, pointing in the direction of the farthest group of boxes near the stairs.

Tyler's cheek was on fire, and he tried to determine what the hell the man was pointing at. Slowly it came into focus. At first it appeared to be a beach ball on top of a chair. He then realized what he was looking at. Tyler felt the vomit rising in his throat.

A clear plastic bag was tightly wrapped around the head of the seemingly embalmed body of Mrs. Larsson. Underneath the plastic, he could just make out her short black hair and two white patches covering her eyes. She looked quite young. She was dressed in what appeared to be a faded white wedding dress, and she was propped up in a large blue chair. Like Tyler, her arms were pulled behind her back, and Tyler could see chains around her ankles. It was at that moment that Tyler knew how he would die.

It was also at that moment that the generator began to sputter and then try to feebly revive itself. It coughed and strained and eventually stopped entirely. The sudden silence was thick, and Tyler caught the look of confusion on the man's face as the room faded to black.

Tyler listened for any movement. He could hear the man breathing, apparently deciding on his next course of action. Tyler realized it was nighttime, as no light came in from either of the two windows. He waited. His heart was racing, and he could feel the adrenaline surging through his body.

He then heard the man shuffling toward the staircase, obviously feeling his way through the dark room. If the generator was indeed out of gas, *Daddy might need to take a bike ride tonight…*

Tyler listened and waited. He heard the man slowly ascending the stairs, then the footsteps above him walking through the kitchen and out toward the living room. *Do it,* Tyler thought, willing the man to leave the house so he could buy some time to figure a way out of this hellhole.

He closed his eyes and waited. After a few excruciating seconds, he heard the front door close. Tyler let out a breath, then quickly lunged forward, lying back down on his stomach, pretending to be unconscious. His eyes remained wide open, facing away from the dark window with the cables running through it. Sure enough, he could see the light of a flashlight illuminating the room through the open basement window at the back of the house. The entire room lit up, and he could see the beam was now pointing in his direction. Tyler remained motionless. *Daddy is checking on me one more time.* Then suddenly the room went dark, and he heard the sound of a squeaky bicycle wheel moving away from the back of the house.

Tyler waited for a minute; then, after a few unsuccessful attempts, he rolled over and managed to get onto his knees. His next move was to shuffle himself backward on his bare knees toward the rope that was attached to the chains on his ankles. Soon he could feel the thick rope beneath his shins. With great difficulty, he continued to wiggle himself backward until he felt the pole bumping against the heel of his right foot.

Tyler moved to one side until he was sure the pole was directly behind both heels. He then leaned forward, attempting to get his feet straight beneath him, and pressed his heels both against his butt and the pole. He leaned even further down until his forehead was on the concrete. Tyler took two deep breaths, braced himself, and then threw himself backward.

His back hit the pole hard, and using his momentum, he instantly pressed all his weight against it, transferring his energy down to his legs and feet. He quickly steadied himself into a standing position. His entire body screamed in pain, and it was all he could do to remain upright. With his hands behind him, he felt for the pole and grabbed it, holding himself against the cold metal. His knees were shaking terribly, and he again thought he would pass out.

By leaning forward slightly, Tyler was able to move his hands up the pole a bit. He knew the crank for the pulley system was somewhere on the pole. Soon he felt it, just behind his elbows. He leaned forward further until his hands could touch the handle and gears. He then searched for a spot that would best allow him to create friction. *The bar holding the handle should work*, he thought, and he pulled his hands over the handle until the plastic connecting both cuffs together was lying over it. He then began working his hands back and forth, allowing the plastic strap to rub against the bar. He was dripping with sweat and quickly running out of breath. He knew that this was going to take every ounce of energy that he had left.

Tyler was getting very dizzy now and beginning to wobble. Without any light, he was struggling to keep his balance and maintain perspective, which made standing on two tightly bound feet almost impossible. He had to occasionally stop to right himself and catch his breath. He could feel the plastic on his wrists getting warmer, and he was soaked with perspiration.

Then suddenly...*snap!*

Tyler's arms shot forward to his side. The pain in his shoulders was overwhelming, and he could feel himself losing consciousness. He was just able to get down to his knees before he passed out on the cold floor.

CHAPTER THIRTY-FOUR

H e was lying on his stomach. It was cold. He was completely naked. Everything slowly began to come back to him. So too did the burning pain in his ankles and shoulders. Everything was dark and disturbingly quiet—very quiet.

Larsson hasn't returned yet—

Tyler knew he needed to work fast. He tried to push himself up, but his arms were incredibly weak, and he collapsed again.

Come on, Tyler, he thought, in full panic mode. *You have to do this.*

He pushed himself over to his side and eventually maneuvered up to a sitting position. He pulled his legs toward his chest and fumbled with the tight chains binding his ankles. Tyler could feel a knot tying the rope to a metal ring that was in turn connected to the chains holding them together. To his delight, the ring felt like a lightweight carabiner, something he had often used for rappelling. He knew that it could be undone by merely unscrewing the screw gate on the straight side of the D-ring.

Moving his hands over the knot, he recognized it as a simple clove hitch. Now with no load on it, Tyler loosened the knot from the carabiner so he could make room for his fingers to unscrew the locking mechanism. His heart sank. The carabiner felt slightly bent. The screw would not budge, no matter how hard he tried. He had to figure out a way to pry back the side used for fastening the carabiner so he could unscrew it. Just then, and to his horror, he could just make out the sound of a squeaky bicycle wheel coming up the driveway toward the back of the house.

Tyler dove forward, getting back into his original position, facedown on the floor. A few seconds later, he saw a light coming from the direction of the window; it again illuminated the entire room. Tyler stayed still, trying to control his heavy breathing. Across the room, he could see the late Mrs. Larsson with her white eye patches, sitting in her wedding dress. He could also see the small wooden stool about three feet from him.

As soon as the light disappeared, Tyler got onto his hands and knees and crawled in the direction of where he had seen the stool. He reached up until he felt one of the stool legs. He dragged the stool toward him. At the same time, he hitched himself back toward the pole.

Tyler then forced himself upright, sitting up and turning the stool onto its side. He pressed all his weight onto one of the top legs, feeling it move slightly. Tyler's arms were weak, and his shoulders were screaming in pain from being tied behind his back for so long, but he continued to push down on the leg until he could feel it begin to loosen. Tyler lunged his body down on top of it, painfully slamming his shoulder onto the leg. *Almost there—*

He sat back up and turned his shoulder toward it again, propelling his body downward. He could feel the leg give way and separate from the bottom of the stool with a resounding *CRACK!* The sound echoed throughout the basement, and Tyler froze, listening in fear until it dissipated.

He quickly felt for the narrower end of the stool leg and, with one hand, directed it into the middle of the carabiner that secured the chains around his ankle. He shifted around until he could feel the metal pole against his feet. Using the pole as leverage and the stool leg as a primitive cheater bar, he began jamming his arms forward around the pole, attempting to force the metal clip back toward its original position. With each push, an unbearable pain shot through his ankles and up his body, threatening to send him into unconsciousness.

Tyler knew he had very little time. He also knew he had no other choice than to keep his focus and continue. He repeatedly rammed the wooden leg forward toward the pole, having no clue if it was working or not.

Suddenly he could hear the unmistakable moan of the generator rumbling to life. The lights above him flickered at first and then exploded into blinding brightness. He could just hear the muffled sounds of children singing high above him.

After pulling the wooden leg out from the carabiner, he reached down toward the screw. His hands were shaking so badly he could hardly grab it. *Come on, Tyler.* He pulled his hands away, closed his fists to get some feeling back into his fingers, then tried again. He managed to grasp it, squeezing with all his might. At the same time, he let out a primal howl as he turned the screw toward him.

It moved slightly at first, began to loosen, and then quickly spun down the thread.

Once undone, Tyler released the carabiner, kicking his legs violently until the chains fell off. His ankles were raw, and there was blood everywhere around him. Without looking back at the stairs, Tyler hobbled over to the open window, screaming in pain with each step. He saw his daypack below it and, remembering his hunting knife was in it, picked it up and quickly put it on. After a couple of failed attempts, he was barely able to haul himself up and through the window.

Using his elbows, he pulled himself forward into the long grass and nettles behind the house. He could feel the gnarly weeds cutting at his naked skin. He managed to force himself to his knees and, with great difficulty, eventually stand. He was wobbling terribly and almost fell over again. Throwing his arms out wide to maintain his balance, Tyler focused on moving one step at a time toward the backyard of the rancher next door. He felt as though he was hardly moving, staggering like a drunk man across the yard.

Despite being completely exhausted, Tyler resisted the temptation to enter the rancher next door. He saw the blood all over his body, and he knew he could be easily tracked by the marks he would leave on the concrete patio. He needed to keep moving.

He could just make out the five-foot-high wooden fence at the far side of the property, dividing it from the duplex next to it. He slowly shuffled his way toward it, feeling like he was in one of those nightmarish dreams where you're running in slow motion and gaining no ground. Eventually, he reached the fence, and he grabbed onto the top of it. With every ounce of energy he could muster, he hoisted himself up, again screaming out in pain. Tyler then shifted his weight forward, feeling himself falling over to the other side and into the tall weeds below. He was done.

CHAPTER THIRTY-FIVE

When Tyler awoke, the morning sun was high in the sky. It took him a while to gather his senses. He could feel the heat of the sun on his naked skin. He looked down and saw that he was covered in blood and had deep scratches all over his body from the brambles. He could see the raw flesh around both ankles. Two plastic zip ties were still tightly secured around both wrists.

Behind him, he heard the familiar drone of the generator nearby. Above the weeds, he could see the top of a rotting wooden fence with what appeared to be streaks of his dried blood down the side. His body felt as if it had been in a car accident, and any movement was torturous. Soon everything started to come back to him, including his fear.

Painfully rolling onto his side, he pressed his back against the warm fence and, ever so slowly, managed to maneuver himself to his knees. He was in agony, but he forced himself up until he could just peer over the fence to the backyard of the rancher and to the little house of horrors beyond it.

He noticed the bike was no longer leaning against the back wall. *Is Daddy out looking for me?*

All was still.

Tyler suddenly remembered his daypack and felt for it on his back.

Still there.

He was comforted to know he now had his hunting knife. He then turned and painfully limped toward the side of the duplex, remaining below the height of the fence. He could see Langer Road ahead of him bathed in sunshine, and he moved forward until he reached the front corner of the house.

Looking to the right, he could see the yellow generator two doors down. Tyler moved forward and, staying in the tall grass close to the house, began to make his way north on Langer. In his condition, and being barefoot, he knew it would take him over an hour before he'd be able to reach his pile of winter clothing, the portal—and freedom. It seemed as though he'd been in West Heights, Ohio, for forever.

CHAPTER THIRTY-SIX

Before venturing out to the road, Tyler decided to remain hidden beneath a tall beech tree within sight of his clothing. He crouched low in the tall grass. He could thankfully see his boots and parka about forty feet away. It was all he could do to restrain himself from bolting toward them, but he wanted to make sure he had remained unobserved.

He listened for any kind of sound or indication that he had been followed. All he could hear was the wind gently tapping the screen door against the frame of the vacant house beside him. Tyler decided it was safe and stood up. Stepping over the skeleton of a small dog, he slowly limped out toward Langer Road.

Tyler was still some fifteen feet away from his clothes when, to his horror, he heard the familiar sound of a squeaky wheel approaching from behind. He quickly spun around. His blood ran cold.

The man was about fifty feet away and rapidly closing the distance. He was steering his bike with one hand and had the tranquilizer gun in the other, resting it on the handlebars in front of him. The weapon was pointing directly at Tyler.

And the man was pedaling very quickly.

Tyler prayed that the man was still too far away to get any kind of accurate shot. He turned and hobbled as fast as he could.

Ten more feet…

Come on, Tyler—

Five more feet…two more feet…

The squeaking was loud now. He could hear the man yelling something at him. He then heard the muffled report of a weapon firing.

Tyler bent down and, in a single motion, scooped up his clothing with both hands and dove headlong toward the pavement beyond.

CHAPTER THIRTY-SEVEN

It was another "This is why I live in Montana" kind of day, and Westy looked up at the azure sky and white peaks of the Bitterroot Mountains. He had opted for a walk around campus rather than lunch in the teachers' lounge. He couldn't stop thinking of Tyler, knowing he had now been gone for nearly a week.

The city of Missoula was a small town in many ways, and people were talking about it everywhere. The rumor mill was alive and well. *Did you hear? A professor with mental issues is missing.*

Westy decided to call Cynthia to give her an update on their excursion out to Tyler's Jeep. Cynthia sounded a little distracted. He figured she was with a client, and after a few pleasantries, he hung up.

Fiddling with the phone in his pocket, Westy toyed with the idea of leaving yet another message on Tyler's cell. He decided against it and headed back to the main building. Tyler would call him when he was good and ready.

Or desperate, he thought as he bounded up the steps.

CHAPTER THIRTY-EIGHT

The jolt of cold snow brought immediate relief to his broken body. Tyler lay for a few seconds on his stomach, face buried beneath the powder, soaking in the soothing sensation on his hot, tattered skin. He slowly lifted his head and listened.

Blissful silence.

The comforting sensation of snow on his body soon became a numbing pain, reminding him that he was still naked.

Tyler sat up and scrambled to find his snow pants, pulling them up and over his legs. They were still warm from the Ohio sun. He then followed with his boots, gingerly pulling them over his throbbing ankles. He took off his daypack and finished dressing, forcing himself to stand despite being virtually devoid of all energy.

It took everything he had to drag himself over toward the fire pit. He assembled some bark and twigs from his small woodpile and dug into his parka for the lighter. His hands were trembling horribly, and it was difficult to ignite it, but before long he had a small flame going. He collapsed to his knees beside it.

He added a small log and watched the hot embers slowly rise to the blue sky above. Tyler sat motionless, staring vacantly at the flames. He was emotionally, physically, and mentally spent.

But he was free.

CHAPTER THIRTY-NINE

The sun was bright and the air crisp, the way winter days should be. The entire city seemed to glow, and the mountains surrounding Missoula appeared to be only a few feet away. Skiing and snowmobiling were on the minds of many of the locals.

Cynthia walked out of the front doors of the hospital, put on her sunglasses, and headed to her car. She had spent the past few hours consulting with doctors and nurses as well as calling her father's oncologist. The last hour had been spent with her parents in a cramped room.

"*Húdié*," her father had whispered when he saw her walk in. "My butterfly." He had smiled weakly and reached out to her. She had melted into his arms, breathing in his familiar scent, one she had known her entire life. The smell of comfort, protection, warmth, and home. She felt his bony chest beneath her head and could hear the congestion in his lungs. Her mother sat silently on the other side of the bed. Cynthia was at a loss for words.

C.W Johnston

CHAPTER FORTY

Tyler spent most of the afternoon just staring at the fire. He would occasionally toss a log on, but he could bring himself to do little else. At one point, he did manage to drag his sleeping bag out of his tent and wrap it around his shoulders for warmth, but that took everything out of him.

It was beginning to get dark and much colder. Tyler knew he desperately needed some sustenance. Eventually, he summoned enough energy to throw some snow into the kettle and bring it to a boil. Once it had cooled enough to drink, he shakily filled his water bottle and slowly sipped the soothing, warm liquid. Despite the pain of swallowing, he emptied it twice.

His spirits lifting a bit, he scooped a few handfuls of snow into his cooking pot and shoved it directly onto the fire. He stumbled over to his pack and pulled out two large packets of freeze-dried casserole, emptying them into the steaming pot. While he waited for it to boil, he took out his

Swiss Army knife from the pack pocket and gently cut both plastic zip-tie cuffs from his raw wrists and threw them into the fire, watching them melt and disappear.

The stars were just becoming visible when Tyler dug out a large spoon from his pack and pulled the pot off the fire with his heavy mitts, placing it on the snow between his legs. This would be the first substantial meal he had had in days.

*

Before heading into his tent for the night, Tyler took out his medical kit and, using the ample firelight to see, carefully cleaned and rubbed all of his wounds with antibacterial ointment. He put bandages and dressings on the more severe abrasions and cuts, quickly covering the exposed part of his body after each application to keep warm. His ankles were by far the worst, the flesh mangled and very painful to touch. He delicately cleaned and wrapped both ankles with white medical gauze.

With a full belly and some relief to his wounds, Tyler crawled into his tent and buried himself deep within his sleeping bag. He was asleep within seconds.

Figment

CHAPTER FORTY-ONE

The next day, Sheriff Patychuk called Diane. It had been nearly a week since Tyler had taken off on his "vacation." He was planning to initiate the first phase of a search in a day or two. He wanted to check in to see if she or Westy had heard anything. She assured him that they hadn't, though she admitted that they had gone out to see the Jeep for themselves. Patychuk had grunted his displeasure. *Damn city folk*, he thought. He made her promise they would call him immediately if they heard anything.

*

Cynthia cancelled all of her appointments for the next couple of weeks. She wanted to spend as much time with her parents as possible. She filled Moses's cat bowl with kibble, grabbed her jacket, and headed to the door. She would be at the hospital in fifteen minutes.

Figment

*

He was stiff and sore, and, judging by how high the sun was in the sky, he had apparently slept uninterrupted for at least twelve hours. Tyler emerged from his tent and hobbled toward the fire pit. He soon had it blazing away again. He spent the rest of the day consuming food and water, treating his wounds, napping, and gathering wood.

By the time he went to bed again, his spirits were higher than they had been in years.

CHAPTER FORTY-TWO

T yler had the fire going by 9:00 a.m. He was moving less gingerly now and felt that much of his energy had returned. He redressed his wounds and was happy to see everything was beginning to heal. He felt confident that he would be ready to pack up and descend the mountain by tomorrow.

After a hearty breakfast, he chopped enough wood to last the day and evening. As he piled it beside the fire, he glanced over toward the alders. His stomach clenched at the thought of what lay beyond those trees.

Even though his phone was powered off, that hadn't stopped it from coming alive in the past. He wondered why all was quiet now.

He thought of the girl with the eye patches and how she had reacted when he had yelled "This train is bound for glory." He had known at that moment that it was she who had been communicating with him. Why hadn't she contacted him since he had returned? *No text, photos…nothing.*

He then remembered the smile on her face when he had last seen her. *She knows I understand what needs to be done,* Tyler thought, moving back toward the fire.

CHAPTER FORTY-THREE

The incident commander of the Missoula County search-and-rescue team had been informed by Sheriff Patychuk about the possibility of an impending search. The team was a highly trained and dedicated group of volunteers, and having a bit of time to prepare was important for everyone.

Patychuk had approved the timing of his two-phase plan. The first stage would commence in two days, beginning with a series of snowmobile and pedestrian searches triangulating outward from Stevens's presumed last location—his Jeep found on the logging road.

The direction of these searches would then be graded according to personality characteristics—in other words, understanding that based on what was learned from Dr. Cynthia Chan, Tyler would most likely have headed in the direction of Whisper Ridge in the Bitterroot Mountains as opposed to away from it. The incident commander would draw an imaginary 180-degree line from Tyler's vehicle facing Whisper Ridge. Each search would gradually spread out from this center point. After all, there was no reason to believe Mr. Stevens had actually made it to the ridge. *Probably dead in a ravine somewhere, frozen solid*, Patychuk thought, pulling his cruiser into the Florence Coffee Company drive-through.

Depending on the result of these searches, the second step could be the initiation of alpine and backcountry teams that could be sent into more hazardous areas. They were experts in avalanche rescues and wilderness first aid. This would be the group that would either rescue Tyler Stevens or recover his remains.

*

The next day, Cynthia and her mom were at the hospital early. When she arrived at her dad's room, Dr. Fortson was just coming out. He signaled to them both to follow him to his office down the hall.

His previous diagnosis may have been a little too optimistic. The latest tests indicated that Mr. Chan's cancer had spread faster than he had anticipated. It was time to suggest that he be moved to the hospice wing connected to the north side of the hospital.

Dr. Fortson had given these talks a thousand times. He would shrug and say, "Hard to say," when they would inevitably ask him how long he might have. Though he knew perfectly well that it probably wouldn't be more than a week or two.

*

The next morning, Tyler rose just after dawn and built his last fire on Whisper Ridge. Once his kettle came to a boil, he stirred a pouch of freeze-dried biscuits and gravy into his large metal mug and sat down on the log where it had all started. He mixed the lumpy mixture together with his spoon. It was moving day, and he dearly hoped he would never have to see this ridge again.

Tyler was packed up and ready to leave his campsite by ten. His ankles were still extraordinarily tender, but he knew that although the descent would be long, it was easy enough with his snowshoes to switch-back his way down. Once his pack was on his shoulders, he didn't look back.

*

It was a much milder day, and the sidewalks were bare, making it easier to walk her mother to the car. There was so much to think of, organize, and arrange; Cynthia was overwhelmed.

Cynthia had not known her grandparents, and she had never lost an uncle, cousin, or friend. Death had never been a part of her immediate experience. She felt utterly empty and drained. She knew she had to be there for her mother and was sure she needed her mom as well. They were all each other had.

She opened the car door for her mother, then stopped and hugged her close. For some reason, Cynthia thought of Tyler Stevens as an eight-year-old, what it would have been like for him to hear the devastating news that both his parents were dead and his older sister was in a coma. She still couldn't fathom how a young boy could have coped with it all.

*

Later that afternoon, Westy and Diane learned that the search-and-rescue team would be assembling in fifteen hours. Diane called Sheriff Patychuk to ask if there was anything they could possibly do to help. The suspense was killing them, and they would happily take the day off work to join the search. The sheriff bluntly declined their kind offer, telling them it was time the professionals were given room to do their jobs.

Westy had just hung up when his cell phone rang. It was Tyler.

CHAPTER FORTY-FOUR

He had reached his Jeep by late afternoon. There were lots of snowmobile and snowshoe tracks all around, and Tyler was sure his vehicle would have been reported. He opened the door. There was an envelope on the dash. He recognized the handwriting and opened it to find the note from Diane.

He read her beautiful words of support and love and her hope for his safe return. Tyler was overcome with emotion. He pulled out his cell phone and turned it on. It instantly began pinging with dozens of text messages and voicemail notifications. He could see most of them were from Diane and Westy.

"Hey, it's me."

"Tyler? Oh, my God! Buddy, is that really you?"

Tyler could hear Diane's muffled gasp in the background.

"Diane's here with me—I'm putting you on speaker phone. Where the hell are you? Are you okay?"

Tyler felt his emotions rising in his throat. "I'm fine, Westy. Thanks for the note, Diane."

"Hi, Tyler." Diane's voice was shaky. "We were *so* worried. Jesus, Tyler—where are you now?"

"I just managed to get this old boy through the snow and am pulling onto RR1. Should be on the highway in about ten. I miss you guys."

"You were on Whisper Ridge, weren't you?" Westy blurted out.

Tyler smiled. "I was. Needed to spend some time there. I'm done now, and it's good to be home. Someday I'll tell you all about it," he lied.

"The bloody SAR were going to head out your way in the morning. Your timing is impeccable." Westy laughed. "I'll call the sheriff back right now. So, when can we see you?"

"Soon," Tyler replied. "I need a few days to get back on my feet." *Literally*, he thought, knowing he was still a few days from walking without a limp. "Thanks for caring, you two. I love you both so much. Please call off the hounds and tell everyone I'm fine and thankful."

Tyler hung up and slowly began to weep. The feeling of being loved was unlike any other.

Figment

CHAPTER FORTY-FIVE

Diane immediately called Dr. Chan and left a message saying that Tyler had resurfaced. She then poured herself another glass of red and handed the bottle to Westy, who had just hung up his phone after speaking with the sheriff's office.

"So why do you really think he needed to go up there again?"

"The ridge? Damned if I know," Westy replied. "Perhaps he just hates unfinished business. He's a bit of a perfectionist that way. In September he had to leave because he was sick, and now he needed to finish the job, so to speak."

"For a week? In the middle of winter?" Diane asked, unsatisfied with his response. "Do you think he found whatever...or whoever he was looking for?"

"Well, we know he's not well. He's struggling. I suppose when he's good and ready he'll tell us. Until then, here's to his return." Westy lifted his glass to Diane's.

Figment

C.W Johnston

PART FOUR

C.W Johnston

CHAPTER FORTY-SIX
February 28th, 2020

Tyler's first few days were spent taking long baths, stocking his fridge, treating his ankle wounds, eating, and napping. Being back at his apartment was unbelievably comforting, and he could feel his body recovering rapidly and his mood brightening. His nights were also blissful; there had not been a single "communication." As much as he wanted to think it all may have been a dream, his throbbing ankles soon pulled him back to reality.

He had called Westy and Diane a bunch of times to assure them that he was okay. They said they understood that he needed some space right now. He was sure they didn't.

As painful as it was to reflect on his experience, Tyler wanted to get it all down while still fresh in his memory. He needed to create a list of the key points of his experience in West "Amityville Horror" Heights. He sat on his couch with his laptop and opened up an Excel document.

He decided to only focus on the key nuggets of information, points that would be valuable for further investigation. He needed to be absolutely certain. He knew he didn't have much time.

*

Close to five days had passed since Tyler had mysteriously returned. Sheriff Patychuk happened to be in the area and decided to drop by to check on him. Truth be told, he was a little pissed off that he had only been a few hours away from sending the boys up that mountain. He hated risking the lives of volunteers on the SAR team, and he felt like giving Mr. Stevens a little piece of his mind—or at the very least, a lesson on courtesy.

He saw Tyler's red Jeep in the driveway. Patychuk pulled in behind it and soon had huffed and puffed his way up the steep stairs to his apartment. He paused briefly to catch his breath at the top, then banged on Tyler's door.

"Who is it?"

Patychuk could hear him walking toward the door. "Sheriff Patychuk. I wouldn't mind a word, if you have a minute."

Tyler slowly opened the door. Patychuk quickly noticed how athletic Stevens looked, remembering his prowess as an outdoorsman. He also noticed that Tyler appeared to be anxious.

"Well, you caused quite a stir down here, Mr. Stevens. Almost had to send a team up there to look for you, you know."

Tyler's smile seemed strained. "I'm sorry, Sheriff. I was gone longer than I had intended. It won't happen again. I promise."

"Well, what were you doing up there, anyway? By Christ, that was a nasty storm we had." Patychuk looked past Stevens and could see a spattering of medical supplies spread across the kitchen counter.

"Yes, it was a doozy. It was beautiful up there, though, so I didn't mind. Well, thanks for checking in, Sheriff. I'm sorry if I caused you any inconvenience."

"You hurt yourself?" Patychuk lifted his head in the direction of the array of bandages, tape, and ointments behind Tyler.

"What?" Tyler turned around. "Oh, that. No, just some silly scratches." Tyler moved toward the center of the door to block the sheriff's view behind him. "So, anything else I can do for you, sir?"

Patychuk grinned. "Naw. Nothing, son, just wanted you to know the boys were primed and ready to roll last weekend. I'm surprised a man of your experience didn't put a protocol in place."

"You're right, sir. I usually do. As I said, I was gone longer than intended." Tyler paused, then reached out and offered the sheriff a handshake.

"Right." Sheriff Patychuk took the cue, smiled weakly, and then shook Tyler's large hand, noticing the strange red welts on his wrist. "Well, I'm glad you're back safely. You have yourself a nice day." Patychuk turned and left. Something didn't sit right with him, but he couldn't put his finger on it. Tyler Stevens seemed distracted. Like he was hiding something.

CHAPTER FORTY-SEVEN

Tyler looked down at his Excel spreadsheet and began to type some headings, giving each one its own page. He narrowed it down to thirteen points.

- Dr. Elias Larsson

- Mrs. Angel Larsson

- His daughter (and Angel's?)—12 or 13 years old

- 337 Langer Road, West Heights, Cuyahoga County, Ohio

- March 16, 2020—Event occurred based on calendar on school wall, etc.

- Estimate 2025 portal visit

- Mr. David Sommerville, 34 Langer Road, West Heights, Cuyahoga County, Ohio (military dress, gas mask)

- Borden on Marigold Avenue, West Heights, Ohio

- Songs about bumble bees, dungarees, and barking dogs. *Hippity Hopping*…a children's live album?

- Vials of antivirus? Tanger?

- Aerovirology

- Seven days (counter on Larsson's video)

- Virus/disease/gas that could cause the sudden death of all life-forms on earth in seven days?

Tyler slowly let out his breath and looked at his list. He would start with his captor, the murderous and clearly psychopathic Dr. Elias Larsson. He felt confident that all roads would lead directly back to him. Tyler's hands began to tremble as he typed his name into Google.

*

It was surprisingly difficult to find any information on Dr. Elias Larsson of West Heights, Ohio. Tyler surmised his work at Borden was secretive. Nonetheless, it was frustrating.

He figured that in this technological age, everyone left some kind of a digital footprint. It was difficult to remain hidden unless you desperately wanted it that way. This guy obviously had a privacy fetish.

He thought of Larsson and his commute each day.

Old school. No car for Dr. Elias Larsson. No, it was an old upright bike, pant clips, and a lunch bucket. *Oh, and panniers to boot.* Tyler remembered how stark his house had been and its 1980s furniture. In fact, he didn't remember even seeing a television. This dude was off the grid.

What made you so special, Dr. Larsson? What made you need to remain so private?

Tyler then remembered what Elias Larsson had said to him just before jabbing him with a needle. "I'm good with chemicals, you know…"

*

The lack of information held true for his wife, Angel Larsson. Nothing about her or their marriage appeared anywhere. *Probably because he knocked her off, stuffed her full of chemicals, and stuck her in his basement before she could so much as say the word* Instagram.

Even odder was that Borden was not listed anywhere. It had no presence on the internet. Was this because of the military connection? Tyler remembered the Department of Defense insignia on the Borden sign. It actually made sense, considering what they were doing there. Did Borden need to remain anonymous? Did they want the world to pass them by so they could quietly play with their poisonous concoctions?

There had only been a discreet sign beside the gate on a quiet suburban street in Nowhere, Ohio. Who would ever have suspected them?

*

Tyler felt he could safely assume his portal visit put him in West Heights somewhere around the year 2025. He assumed this based on two observations: the bones and the girl.

Considering the complete decomposition of the skeletal remains as well as the decay and overall abandoned state of West Heights during his time there, he thought at least a few years must have passed.

Tyler then thought of the wretched girl with the eye patches. He did the math in his head. If she was around twelve years of age when he saw her, and if the event had occurred in 2020, then she must have been born around 2013. So she must have been around seven years old when the event occurred—give or take a year or so.

In all the futuristic movies he had ever seen, people tended to travel a long way into the future. Not five years. *Seems almost like a missed opportunity*, he thought sarcastically.

Tyler again considered the "event" on March 16th, 2020. The magnitude of it all then crashed down on him. He looked at the date at the top of his computer screen, and the reality of what would happen to the world in just over two weeks made him queasy.

He then decided to research David Sommerville of the 34 Langer fame and was relieved to find a plethora of information. Tyler remembered Sommerville's skeleton lying at the top of the stairs, his arms stretched out in front of him, clutching a gas mask.

Sommerville was a military guy. A recruitment officer at the Cleveland recruiting battalion—the Rockstar Battalion, as it was known when Tyler searched for it. As far as he could tell, Sommerville had no connection to Borden. Facebook and LinkedIn suggested he was single and that he liked to golf, go to airplane shows, and listen to country music. Tyler moved on down the list.

The only live children's record he could find that seemed to have all components of the lyrics and songs he'd heard at 337 Langer was by a group called The Sunny Skies and Smiles Trio. The album was called *Happy Times!* and was released in 1962.

Tyler opened up Apple Music and did a search. Finding *Turn around and Jump Down*, he pressed play. It was undoubtedly the same album. He immediately turned it off. He never wanted to hear any of those songs or the laughter again.

Tyler quickly scanned the song titles. He felt a chill go through his entire body when he got to the last song on the album. There were two words: "This Train."

"Jesus Christ," Tyler exclaimed loudly, trying to digest that nugget. "What the hell?"

He tried to get his head around how the song he had played that fateful night last fall on Whisper Ridge—a song that he had played since before he could remember—just so happened to be on Daddy's favorite album? "Fuck me," Tyler blurted out. Tyler felt that familiar pounding in his chest and knot in his stomach.

Deep down, he knew it wasn't merely by chance. There was meaning in this coincidence. There was purpose. Synchronicity.

Tyler thought of the girl lying in bed with her eye patches, forced to listen to that album relentlessly on repeat and at full volume. Day after day, year after year—an endless barrage. The torturous, twisted life she had endured was beyond his ability to grasp.

How long had she waited for him? What were the chances of him appearing on that particular ridge on that weekend? He thought about how time might work in her dimension. Perhaps she had been in a holding pattern until all the stars had aligned.

Tyler remembered how odd it was that the length of days in both realities seemed to be about the same— morning on the ridge was morning in West Heights. Yet both realities were in different seasons, not to mention different decades. Like everything else he was experiencing lately, it was pretty fucked up.

Tyler recalled an event he had helped organize for his university in an attempt to raise its academic profile. He had decided to arrange a debate on the very existence of God, without formally using the name God—to keep the more conservative members of the university happy. He used the prompt: "Is there any will or meaning behind what happens?" In other words, is there a designer behind the design?

On one team, two professors who were quite religious agreed to debate the topic. Their opposition for the event were a couple of science professors who were self-professed atheists.

They all had a month to prepare, and on the night of the event, over three hundred students and faculty came to watch the good-hearted exchange. The atheists had the easier task, as they could lean on facts. The two science professors used all the common jargon and theories to build their case. They belittled the belief in fairies and waxed lyrical about the virtues of scientific data versus false information, false prophets, and faith.

Interestingly, the religious professors also used science and logic in their argument, bringing out all sorts of data designed to show the implausibility of random chance being responsible for the intricacies of life. They explored life at the basic molecular level and set up their case based on statistics and design.

Their basic premise was that the sheer complexity of the design of life could not have simply happened by chance. They argued that the statistical likelihood of that occurring would be the same as a tornado whirling through a junkyard and, when the dust cleared, a fully functional 747 airplane would be sitting there in the middle of the yard. That would mean every nut and bolt was in place, all the seats lined up in neat, identical rows, and all the electronics and mechanics—all of it—would be flight-ready at the end of the storm. Who would believe this could be possible? Statistically, this was the same as life as we know it randomly coming into existence. Nonsense!

They ended their convincing presentation with the declaration that there must have been will and meaning behind the creation of life—it could not possibly have occurred randomly, as it is too complex; purpose and intelligent design were the only logical explanation.

The crowd had been swayed and applauded appreciatively. Whoops and hollers of agreement resounded from the believers scattered throughout the hall.

Tyler had thought the argument was sound and delivered with confidence and aplomb. The religious folks had made a strong case, and it looked like they were on the verge of winning the debate. At least until one hand went up in the back of the lecture hall and a young freshman posed one simple question to the two men representing the affirmative.

Tyler could still visualize him now, nervously standing and clearing his throat.

"But isn't this simply about time?"

Both men looked at each other and then back at the young student. "What do you mean?" one of the religious professors asked with a touch of condemnation.

The freshman continued. "Well, would it not be true that if there was enough time involved, let's say all of eternity"—he paused for effect—"then couldn't it happen? I mean, seriously, if given all of eternity and an endless stream of tornados in that junkyard, then statistically, wouldn't you at least have to concede that, over time, it *could* happen? How could you not, considering we are talking about endless time? Isn't that rather arrogant?"

There had been an immediate murmur in the crowd and then a burst of applause. He had a marvelous point. Random drops of water can eventually erode a mountain, given enough time. The professors knew they had just lost.

Tyler related this to his situation. What if the odds of him being on that ridge, playing that song at that specific time, and being heard by that girl were like the tornado? What if there was an eternity of time for him, or anyone, to head up to that ridge and play that song? Who's to say that time follows the same rules in crazyland?

Tyler again thought of the girl, stuck in time like Sleeping Beauty waiting for her prince. Perhaps things were merely waiting to unfold.

CHAPTER FORTY-EIGHT
March 1st, 2020

The next day, Tyler awoke at five o'clock and decided his ankles had healed enough to go for a quick run. He needed to find some kind of normalcy in all of this pandemonium. He managed a couple of miles. Once back home, he poured a large mug of coffee and wrapped his ankles in ice. Lying on the couch, he opened up his laptop. It was time to dial in again.

He brought up the cover of The Sunny Skies and Smiles Trio album. It featured two young men in yellow suits and bright orange ties, each holding an instrument and standing in front of a single microphone. Surrounding them, a group of children stood smiling.

Totally a photo from the 1960s, Tyler thought, observing the innocence of the scene. He looked again at the date of its release: 1962. Based on the age Tyler felt Larsson appeared to be in West Heights, it was probably around the time he would have been born.

Figment

Was this your favorite album, Dr. Larsson?

*

Cynthia was told chemotherapy and radiation were out of the question. It was much too late for that. His disease was aggressive and had progressed beyond treatment. Cynthia said she wanted a second opinion. They encouraged her to seek one, though they remained confident in their prognosis.

*

Tyler now focused his research on anything to do with antiviruses and aerovirology. Terms he remembered from his brief sojourn into the belly of the Borden complex. He had heard many of these terms in his first year of university when he had thought he would like to get into medicine. He remembered nothing from those freshman courses, and from the look of his internet search, there was too much to digest in one sitting. But he was starting to get the picture.

Tyler figured the copious injections of something called Tanger (he couldn't remember what else had been written on the box in the kitchen) allowed Larsson and his daughter to survive some kind of virus or disease, while all other living things had contracted it rapidly. Whatever it was, it traveled so quickly that the entire planet seemingly succumbed to it in just over seven days—as indicated by the counter at the bottom of Larsson's apocalyptic slideshow.

The injections seemed to have been necessary long after the event, as they were apparently a daily occurrence at Chateau Larsson. Tyler could still picture the bruised arms of the girl as well as the welts all over Larsson's forearms. He wondered why he himself hadn't been affected by it. He deduced that it must have had something to do with initial exposure. Whatever occurred, Larsson and his daughter seemed to still require daily injections of Tanger.

Tyler decided to save the more technical research for the morning. He put his laptop on the couch beside him and leaned back, closing his eyes.

He needed to put a plan together.

It was 3:37, and Tyler's phone was vibrating. He reached for it but realized he had fallen asleep on the couch. He stumbled over to the kitchen to grab it. There was only one word.

Hurry.

CHAPTER FORTY-NINE
March 2nd, 2020

In the morning, Tyler glanced at the date on his phone. He had exactly two weeks. He felt motivated and purposeful and spent most of the day educating himself on pathogens, antigens, viruses, and infectious diseases. He needed to be sure.

He reckoned that whatever had hit West Heights and beyond had been airborne. The way the skeletons were scattered around town, it was apparent something had overcome the city with little warning. *About the time it would take to run down the stairs to grab a gas mask, but not enough time to then put it on*, he thought.

From what he read, there was no virus currently known that could move as quickly and efficiently as what apparently occurred in West Heights. It was obviously not something transmitted by contact or by birds or insects. Equally obvious was that it could not just be carried by the wind—it moved too quickly—which ruled out any type of gas. Whatever it was, it was consistent and constant. If Larsson's slideshow was true, it moved 360 degrees with identical consistency, speed, and ferocity.

Tyler skipped through the more complicated scientific explanations to get a basic understanding of what could have occurred. He knew that air was a mixture of many elements: primarily nitrogen and oxygen, along with things like carbon monoxide, helium, methane, and traces of water vapor. Because of the sheer speed of the transmission in Ohio, he knew that this was no ordinary airborne disease where pathogenic microbes were transmitted by something like sneezing or coughing.

No, this was unlike anything ever seen before. *Ever.*

He suspected that Borden had found a way to transmit a virus by using the equivalent of an unstoppable domino effect. He imagined a virus moving at the molecular level, so it didn't need to rely on wind or transmission by a host; once it was released into the atmosphere, it merely infected air itself. Tyler shuddered at the idea.

He tried to recall the various departments and divisions listed in the foyer of Borden that night he had initially followed Larsson. He closed his eyes and tried to visualize the board. He remembered the first floor had been devoted mostly to general offices, the second to things like epidemiology and analytics. The top level was almost exclusively used for research on viruses and diseases.

Larsson's floor.

Tyler believed that as a director of research, Dr. Larsson would have had full access, and most likely total control, over the third floor of Borden. Tyler knew deep down that whatever had initially occurred in West Heights, and had quickly engulfed the planet, Larsson must have had prior knowledge. How else would he and his daughter have survived? He was complicit. They must have had access to an antivirus—Tanger—*prior* to the event. Tyler remembered the stockpile of boxes stacked high in Larsson's basement.

Tyler wondered if other people had possibly survived? If so, were they involved or in any way responsible for this event? Tyler recalled the disturbing image of the embalmed body of Angel Larsson, perched in a chair and wearing her wedding dress. She had been tortured, then killed by Larsson. Her death had obviously occurred sometime before Ohio-geddon. Was this step one of a larger plan?

It was then that the haunting words Larsson had spoken in the basement came back to him. He could still hear the sickening pride in his high-pitched voice: "I kill everything, you know. It's what I do."

Tyler snapped his laptop closed, thinking again of the text he received last night: *Hurry*.

*

Diane called Tyler just before dinner. She and Westy wanted to drop in briefly with a bottle of wine. They wanted to show him some love and make sure he was okay. They insisted. They wouldn't take no for an answer.

Tyler quickly tidied his apartment and took a shower. While he waited for them to arrive, he checked his emails. There was one from the medical department at Missoula College. It appeared that in order for his leave of absence to be extended, he would need another report from either a doctor or registered psychologist indicating his inability to continue to work. His head of department had also emailed asking if he had any indication of when a return would be likely.

The doorbell rang. Tyler couldn't wait to hug his friends. He had been alone for too long.

Figment

*

As it turned out, Westy and Diane just happened to have brought dinner with them. Tyler smiled, grabbing the takeaway bags of delicious-smelling curry from Westy. Tyler hadn't eaten properly in days, and he was famished. They also happened to bring more than one bottle of wine. They planned to stay.

By the end of the evening, he was exhausted by his own constant deflection and vagueness. Every question they had asked only received half answers or shrugs. Yes, he had spent the entire time camping on the ridge. No, he didn't find anyone else there. Yes, he was satisfied that he found closure up there. Yes, he felt he was getting better. No, he hadn't gotten any weird late-night texts lately. Yes, he was eager to return to work.

Though Diane and Westy were thrilled to have seen him and to let him know they were there for him, they left feeling as confused as they had been when they arrived. Sadly, it appeared that his illness had moved to a different level. He was distant and removed from their conversation the entire night. Without knowing it at the time, both Diane and Westy were thinking the same thing: *What happened up on that mountain that took Tyler away from us?*

CHAPTER FIFTY
March 5th, 2020

Three days after receiving the email from his college, Tyler mustered up the courage to call Dr. Chan. He needed her professional opinion of his incompetence so he could buy himself some time with the college. He also knew that he had to tell her enough to convince her he was still ill, but not enough to have her call in the big boys.

Finally, he just wanted to spend time with her.

"Hey, it's Tyler."

"Tyler." Her voice was gentle. Accepting.

"How's it going?" Small talk was never his strong suit.

"Oh, you know. Busy." Cynthia sounded a little distant.

"Hey, the college wants me to have another meeting with you. You know, to ensure I'm still nuts."

"I see. Are you?"

Tyler thought he could sense Cynthia's smile.

"Maybe just a tad. What works for you?"

"How is tomorrow? Say, nine?"

"Sounds great. Thanks, Doc."

CHAPTER FIFTY-ONE

Tyler had so many questions rattling around in his head and few answers. His questions mostly revolved around the girl. Was she the love child of Angel and Elias Larsson?

The questions always led Tyler back to complete shoulder shrugging, I-don't-have-a-frickin'-clue conclusions. Simple questions, like why the girl contacted him in the first place. And equally important, how the hell was she able to contact him? He remembered Larsson's words when Tyler was trapped in his chamber of horrors. "She is special, you know…"

Did Daddy know his baby girl had a unique ability? Tyler wondered. Was this special quality one that allowed her to communicate back in time? Did it give her superhero powers so she could use fucking radios and phones in another time zone? Was this ability a result of the virus, or whatever the hell it was? Was this why Daddy had only saved her?

Too many questions remained. Tyler's head felt like exploding.

Tyler recalled that the girl must have been around seven or eight years old when the event had occurred. She would have been old enough to recall a world with people. Now the only living person she had was her father. *Christ*, Tyler thought. He tried desperately to get his head around that concept.

Daddy must have had to explain things to her. Tyler imagined what that would have been like for a seven-year-old. What details did he leave out? What did she know?

Was what he told you so disturbing that you needed to send out an SOS?

Finally, he thought about Whisper Ridge. Why there of all places? Did the indigenous people who named it know something about that ridge? What did they experience? Did any of them ever time-travel?

Tyler decided, there and then, that he would dedicate the rest of the day to some serious soul-searching. He needed to unclutter his mind and refocus his thinking. He needed to find the truth and then ultimately commit to doing something about it. Time was quickly running out.

The biggest question of all remained, that of his own sanity. Tyler needed to be completely confident that his experience had been real. He believed he could resolve that question easily with three simple words: *my bloody ankles.*

Unless he had injured his ankles another way and failed to recall it—*highly fucking unlikely*—then they were the real evidence that proved his entire experience was not just a figment of his imagination. He had experienced excruciating pain, and his scars were the proof that something traumatic and authentic had occurred to him. Strangely, this validation seemed to make him feel better.

He dove deeper. So even if this experience was real, this did not confirm that he wasn't mentally ill. Could this bizarre dystopian experience be a construct of his mind? Delusion? In other words, could his mangled ankles be a result of a madman running around the snowy woods on a mountaintop thinking he was in sunny Ohio?

Tyler looked down and rubbed his hands over the tender scars surrounding both ankles. Only a chain could have made those markings. Suddenly he remembered the small chain he had brought to Whisper Ridge for his Dutch oven.

He'd had access to a chain.

But how could he have imagined all of this? *Bullshit.* How could he have possibly known to research all of these things? There were too many meticulous details he had remembered, and now verified, about some place called West Heights, Ohio.

By the end of the day, Tyler convinced himself that what he'd experienced was definitely real. Despite what others might think, it was the truth. It was his truth. And that truth was simple: he had visited the future, and he had witnessed horrible things.

He needed to decide on his next course of action. He opened up his laptop and made some notes. Regardless of how it would unfold, there would be serious ramifications.

CHAPTER FIFTY-TWO
March 6th, 2020

ynthia met him at the door. She noticed he had lost weight. "Good to see you again, Tyler. I'm glad you're safe."

"Thanks, Doc. Usual seat?"

Cynthia smiled. "Coffee?"

"No thanks, I'm good. Had a couple already. How are you doing?" Tyler asked, taking his seat.

Cynthia sat down across from him. "My father is dying. I'm not handling it well. He's very important to me."

"Jesus, I'm so sorry." Tyler was taken aback by her bluntness—it always made him a little off-kilter when he was with her. He envied her ability to remain open and honest, even with her own life. It allowed him to lower his guard. "Cancer?"

Cynthia nodded, tearing up. She forced a smile and changed the subject. "So, Professor Stevens, why don't you tell me about your little adventure up to Whisper Ridge?"

Little adventure? Shit, she is something else. "I hear you connected with my pals Westy and Diane."

"They were worried. I was worried. I didn't betray any confidences."

"They're good people. I didn't mean to worry them." Tyler looked at Cynthia; he could see the concern in her eyes. "Or you."

"They are wonderful people, Tyler. You can learn a lot about a person by the friends they keep." She grinned and tucked her legs up onto her chair. Tyler loved how casual and comfortable she was. "They care a great deal about you."

"So, tell me about your dad." Tyler thought he'd turn the tables on her a bit. He wanted to know a little more about what made her tick. He felt good in her presence, despite his reaction to her during their last visit.

Cynthia smiled warmly. "He is a gentle, kind soul. Worked hard and never complained a day in his life. I have always been his butterfly. He gave me everything."

Tyler could sense Cynthia's pain. "I'm sorry, Cynthia. This is a horrible time for you."

Cynthia nodded. "It's all a part of the circle of life, I guess. Doesn't make it easier, though."

"Well, he raised an amazing woman."

Cynthia forced another smile. "I don't know about that. I seem to remember the last time we met you were pretty upset with me."

Tyler slowly nodded. "You touched a nerve."

"We all have triggers."

"The accident was a long time ago, but it is still very raw."

"It was a devastatingly traumatic event in a young boy's life." Cynthia looked down at her hands. "I have had many amazing years with my dad. A lot of time to build memories. Time to appreciate and know him. You had no such opportunity with your entire family. What you had to deal with is unfathomable."

"It is what it is." Tyler squirmed a little in his seat.

"Perhaps."

"Look, losing my family was obviously horrible. I'm just not sure your inference that it may have impacted my sanity is justified."

"Perhaps not. But it needs to be examined."

Tyler looked directly at her. He knew she was right. She had asked the right questions. "I'm sorry I walked out on you. You were just doing your job."

"Thanks, Tyler." Cynthia smiled and leaned back. "So what's the deal with Whisper Ridge?" Cynthia picked up her notepad and waited.

Tyler paused before responding. This could change everything.

On the one hand, he respected her—even liked her—and wanted to test the waters with her. Perhaps she could give him some perspective and advice. In many ways, he actually wanted to be crazy. It would make things a lot easier.

However, Tyler had already determined what he would tell her and, more importantly, what he would leave out. His story was too phantasmagorical to be believed. Even the thought of telling it made him cringe. Sitting in her office in Missoula seemed a billion miles away from what he had just experienced. There was no way to begin to explain it. Any rational person upon hearing even a portion of his story would think Tyler was a certifiable nutter.

Tyler inhaled deeply before beginning. He had to offer enough to appear genuine, and he certainly didn't want to mislead her. He had too much respect for her. So he started with the obvious: why he returned to the mountain.

He began, "I wanted to find the person that took the picture of me." He then told her about the hike and how he set up the tent in the exact location. Then he explained how he tried to locate the place from where the picture had been taken.

Then he dropped the bomb.

"There is a place on the ridge that allows you to step forward in time."

Cynthia visibly swallowed. She didn't say a thing.

"The messages I have been receiving seem to emanate from there. I don't know how or why, so don't bother asking me. I don't want to go into the details, and *yes*, I know how stupid I sound right now."

Tyler didn't take his gaze off of Cynthia. He could see the bewilderment and confusion in her eyes. "So, in a nutshell, I went up a mountain, and I stepped forward in time. I went in and came back out. I saw the future. Oh, and by the way, it doesn't look good. End of story." Tyler sat back and crossed his legs.

Tyler watched Cynthia attempt to mentally assemble everything she had just heard. She then put down her pen and gradually looked up from her notepad. "The future?"

"Yes."

"When in the future?" she asked, clearly unsure of where this was heading.

Tyler knew this was a tricky one. "Not too far."

"I see," Cynthia said, tilting her head to one side and looking directly at Tyler. He was sincere. He even admitted it sounded absurd, so he was objective about the delusion. She didn't miss a beat. "Tell me, were you able to find the photographer?"

Tyler had expected sarcasm, but there was none; he was impressed by how she had taken it. "I don't want to talk about it."

"Okay. So that's all I get?"

"For now. Just sounds crazy saying it out loud."

Cynthia studied Tyler's face. He was deadly serious.

"So, to recap, you found a way to get into the future, but you don't want to talk about it."

"Correct."

"Okay. So let's say I believe you for now but wouldn't say no to a little more detail. Perhaps some evidence?"

"Evidence?" He thought of his ankles, but there was no way he was going down that path.

"Sure, why not?" she asked calmly. "Something tangible. Something empirical. It's always nice to have a bit of evidence, don't you think?"

Tyler heard her question as another way of saying, *You are talking out of your ass, and I'm going to let you prove it to yourself.*

Tyler smiled. "You want to know if I brought home the moon rocks?"

"Sorry?"

Tyler laughed. "Cynthia, I know you don't think I landed on the metaphorical moon. And no, I don't have moon rocks to prove it to the deniers. I have no evidence, but I know what I experienced." Tyler wanted to be done. He was sure he had given her more than enough to provide him with a medical slip.

Then Tyler stopped smiling. He couldn't believe he hadn't thought of it before.

He actually *did* have evidence.

Tyler grabbed the arms of his chair and leaned forward urgently. "Doc, I think I actually might have some moon rocks."

Cynthia looked confused. "Tyler, I was only—"

Tyler then jumped up and began pacing around her office. His head was swirling, and he could feel his adrenaline kicking in. Cynthia looked at him nervously. He had suddenly become agitated and anxious, but at the same time, extremely excited and happy.

"Look, Cynthia, when I was there—you know, in the future—I saw a little girl. She was just a kid. Probably about twelve or thirteen." Tyler was so wound up, he couldn't control himself.

"She couldn't talk, and she had these eye patches on—anyway, she was the person that had been communicating with me. I'm sure of it." Tyler was talking so quickly that Cynthia could barely keep up as she took notes.

"Anyway, before I left her room, I took a ribbon from the top of her bureau—you know, her chest of drawers. It was sitting on top. A pink one. You know, a hair ribbon. Like what girls wear."

Cynthia gulped softly.

"Anyway, I put it in my jeans that I had taken from—never mind. Then later, I put it in my daypack, along with my flashlight and knife and stuff. It should still be in there." Tyler laughed out loud, feeling vindicated. He threw his arms up in the air and was grinning from ear to ear as if to say, *Case closed.*

Cynthia was gobsmacked. She didn't know how to respond. The sudden change in his behavior had taken her completely off guard. He now appeared to be like a child, happily dancing around her office. He had transformed in front of her eyes. The intensity of his emotional response and his utter conviction was bizarre and completely unnerving.

"I see," Cynthia said weakly. "Tyler, please come and have a seat again. We need to—" Before she could finish the sentence, Tyler was already running out the door.

CHAPTER FIFTY-THREE
March 8th, 2020

A meeting had been requested by the chancellor. Westy was to come down after his last lecture. Her office was on the main floor.

Chancellor Gail Severn's executive assistant waved him through as soon as he arrived. Dr. Severn had been in her position since day one. She was respected and known for the great pride she felt for Missoula College. The last thing she wanted was for MC to obtain any kind of blemish on its reputation.

After the perfunctory niceties, she got down to business. Severn wanted to know what Westy knew about Professor Tyler Stevens. Specifically, how he was doing. She had heard some disturbing things about his mental health.

CHAPTER FIFTY-FOUR
March 10th, 2020

"**D**amn," Tyler yelled, rummaging through the closet in his bedroom for the second time. He then ran back out to the coatrack by the kitchen. Nothing.

"Fuck. Shit, shit, shit." He ran back into the living room and scoured the area. Then it dawned on him—

He remembered now where he had left it.

How the hell could I have been so stupid? His daypack was still on Whisper Ridge. It was probably still lying there by the portal, next to the blood-smeared snow where his naked body had landed. He had taken it off before getting dressed, forgetting to retrieve it before leaving the mountain.

Tyler sat down on his couch and held his head in his hands.

He had no moon rocks after all.

*

The Chinook was a dandy. The "snow-eater" moved in overnight, and suddenly it was spring. They expected a high of over fifty degrees in Missoula today, thanks to the warm winds swooping down from the west.

Westy pulled his car in front of The Budapest and ran up the three flights of stairs to Dr. Chan's office. As a favor, she had come in specifically to see him. He had heard about her dad, and he appreciated her taking the time.

After a few formalities, Cynthia asked him what was going on. Westy was distraught. He wanted to know how to process all of this. He was confused, and she felt a deep sense of loyalty to Tyler.

Cynthia had no answers. It was a difficult thing to stand by someone who was no longer there.

CHAPTER FIFTY-FIVE
March 11th, 2020

Tyler spent most of the night rolling around in his bed, sheets twisting around his body as he desperately attempted to find peace of mind. Tyler dove in and out of a dream state, shivering and drenched in cold sweat.

He felt himself slowly tearing apart. Tyler knew this was all too much for one man to possibly endure. He was, however, adamant about the reality of what he had experienced. He would stand by it until the day he died. Despite this, he longed for the simplicity and sanity of his former life. Why the hell did he have to visit that damn ridge anyway?

Most of all, he was just sad. Sad that this had happened at all. And he was exceedingly regretful about how it would all inevitably unfold.

*

Cynthia Chan decided to go for a run. She rarely ran, but when she did, she usually pushed it. Her mom was still asleep. Cynthia had spent much of the night cuddling her and thanking her for being an amazing mother and wife to her father.

Now she just wanted to run. She was tired of being responsible. The one people always expected to have the answers. She longed for fresh air and freedom. Just for a few minutes.

*

Tyler purchased his return tickets to Ann Arbor online. He then threw on a jacket and walked down the street to the ATM outside The Paw Print. He withdrew five hundred dollars, adding to the nearly two thousand dollars in cash he'd gotten from the bank yesterday. He would only use cash once he landed in Michigan.

He had called his aunt earlier in the day. She sounded as though she was literally shaking with excitement at the thought of his impending visit.

Figment

Tyler pushed through the doors of the pub. He waved at Patty. She knew what kind of beer to bring him.

PART FIVE

Figment

CHAPTER FIFTY-SIX
Monday, March 13th, 2020

The bus ride from Ann Arbor to Cleveland would take just under three hours. The weather was balmy, and Tyler could smell spring in the air. He boarded the bus at noon. He felt surprisingly calm, resolved to focus on the task at hand.

*

After their meeting last week, Cynthia had called Tyler's doctor. Her request for an immediate referral to a specialist was "still in the hopper." She knew that timing would be critical. Tyler was not well and could deteriorate rapidly without treatment.

Cynthia had been shocked by the depth of his psychosis, considering the minimal time it had taken to evolve. He was now acutely delusional and anxious. At the same time, he was both lucid and cordial. He seemed to be able to switch between the two extremes within seconds.

It was as Jekyll and Hyde as she had ever seen.

Cynthia knew how the red tape would work. The system would take time; she hoped, without confidence, that they had already contacted him. While she felt an affinity for Tyler, perhaps even a connection, her work with him was officially done.

Cynthia stroked Moses, who was purring away on her lap, and took another sip of wine. She was experiencing a rare evening at home. The constant visits to the hospital were taking their toll on both her and her mom.

Her mother was asleep in her bedroom. She had been staying with Cynthia full-time lately. It was too hard for her to be alone in a bed she had shared with someone for over forty years.

Cynthia's mind shifted back to her last meeting with Tyler. What the hell was it he said about some girl in a bed?

"She couldn't talk, and she had these eye patches on…"

Cynthia immediately thought of Tyler's sister, who had died so young. She remembered that she had been twelve at the time. She had been lying in a bed in a coma for weeks.

She couldn't see or talk either.

CHAPTER FIFTY-SEVEN
Monday, March 13th, 2020

He arrived at the Cleveland bus station just after 3:00 p.m. He walked directly out the main doors, turning right on Chester Avenue. In ten minutes, he had checked into the nondescript Comfort Motel under the pseudonym Elias Larsson. *Why not?* he thought, unlocking the door to his room.

Like he'd done for the bus ticket, he paid cash for the motel. It would be a thirty-minute taxi drive to West Heights in the morning. Now he needed to calm himself down, focus on his objective, and try to achieve some semblance of sleep.

*

Westy called and left a few messages. He wanted to get Tyler out for some exercise. More importantly, he wanted some answers himself. He had vigorously defended Tyler's mental stability to the chancellor. Now he just needed a little reassurance.

CHAPTER FIFTY-EIGHT
Tuesday, March 14th, 2020

The taxi dropped him off in front of 24 Langer. It was just past seven in the morning. He now stood on the very spot where his portal had been. It seemed a lifetime ago.

Tyler felt sick with the tension.

The entire street was barely recognizable. Though still early spring, the properties looked immaculate. The birds were singing, the lawns were trimmed, and the cars looked bright and shiny. It all seemed so perfectly suburban. *It all looks so different.*

Tyler turned around and walked a few steps.

No portal.

He kept walking, half expecting to fall on his face in the snow.

Nothing.

As he turned around again, he noticed a woman coming out the front door of 24. He recognized her from the picture he had seen in the hallway of her house. She had a little boy in her arms, and she was heading to her car. He could just make out the silver necklace with the locket around her neck.

He felt empty inside. All he wanted to do was run over and hold her. To warn her. To tell her to grab her babies and *get the fuck out of there!*

Tyler realized he had to move. He was a stranger in this neighborhood. He couldn't be seen standing and gawking. He didn't want to look conspicuous, so he picked up the pace and headed south.

He soon came upon 34 Langer Road. He recognized Sommerville's house. There was no car out front today, and Tyler assumed he had already left for work. *Or he's golfing.* Tyler remembered the golf balls in his junk drawer. He walked on.

*

Fifteen minutes later, Tyler had reached the rancher beside 337. More and more people were emerging from their houses and getting into their cars. It was a chilly morning but pleasant for the middle of March in Ohio.

Tyler paused and leaned over, pretending to tie his shoes. He suspected he was a little early; he checked his watch and hoped Larsson had always been a creature of habit. Sure enough, the door opened at quarter to eight.

The man that emerged was much younger looking, but it was definitely him. He had on a red bike helmet and a reflective vest over his dress shirt and was carrying a black lunch bucket. He bent over to put clips around his brown pants.

When the man stood up again, he looked to the right and then left, pausing briefly to glance at Tyler, then moved around the house toward the back. Tyler could hardly breathe.

He needed to time it perfectly, so he began to slowly walk toward 337 until he knew the man would be coming down the driveway on his bike at same time as he would be crossing in front. It was all he could do to hold it together.

Almost immediately the man appeared on his bike. It was a newer model, and Tyler noticed the rear wheel was not squeaking. Larsson slowed down when he saw Tyler standing in front of him.

"Excuse me, sir." Tyler stepped up toward him, forcing a smile. It took everything he had to keep from throwing up. Looking into Larsson's eyes again was torturous.

Larsson slammed on his brakes and put his feet down to steady himself, stopping beside Tyler. He looked annoyed and suspicious. He didn't say anything. He just looked at Tyler, trying to figure out if he knew him.

"Sorry to disturb you. I've just moved into the area. Back there about two blocks." Tyler turned briefly to point north on Langer. "I'm looking for a church for my wife and daughter to attend, and I heard there might be one in the area. Do you know if I'm in the right vicinity?"

Larsson eyed him and slowly shook his head. "Nope."

"Oh well, thanks anyway." Tyler smiled. "Looks like you're heading to work. You work around here?"

Larsson nodded. "The pharmacy. I'm late." The man got back on his bike and began pedaling, turning right on Langer.

Tyler let out a deep breath and watched him disappear. He then turned to look at the house. The curtains were drawn on all of the windows. He knew a young girl could be lying alone in her bedroom on the top floor right now. And there was most likely a very dead Mrs. Larsson sitting in a chair in the basement.

He was deciding what to do next when he saw a couple coming out of the rancher next door. The same one he had used as a hideout for a few days. They looked over at him, waved, and said good morning. They looked to be about his age.

"Oh, hey. Good morning. Do you have a minute? I have a quick question." Tyler greeted them warmly. He was thinking on the fly now.

"Sure," the husband said, walking across the lawn toward him. His wife followed, looking a little suspicious of this stranger in front of the neighbor's house at this hour of the morning.

"Thanks so much. I'm new to the area and was just asking your neighbor there about a church for my wife and daughter to attend. He said he had to get to work, so I didn't get any information from him. He suggested I ask his wife. I was just going to knock at their door. Would she be home?"

"His wife?" the man said, extending his hand toward him. "Dick Shore. This is my wife, Becky. Welcome to the neighborhood."

Tyler shook his hand, then waved at Becky. He didn't give his name.

"He said to ask his wife? That's odd, as we haven't ever seen a wife," Becky said bluntly, looking up at her husband. It was apparent they were confused.

"Oh, that *is* odd," Tyler replied. *Probably because she's stone-cold dead and currently sitting in her wedding dress in the basement next door.*

Dick and Becky exchanged a quick glance. It was Dick who replied. "Not really sure about a wife. Rumor has it, he had a little something-something with his housekeeper. She was younger than him. By at least twenty years. Pretty girl. I heard through the grapevine she might have even been pregnant by him."

The girl, Tyler thought.

"But we haven't seen any wife, pregnant or not," Becky added.

"I must say, he didn't seem the friendliest chap just now." Tyler was digging for more information, but he didn't want to appear too interested.

"Can't say. Don't really know him," Dick said. "Keeps to himself mostly. Only see him in the morning and evening on that bike, wearing that silly vest."

"No, he's not," Becky intervened with conviction.

"Not friendly?" Tyler asked.

"There's always lots of yelling and screaming coming from that place. It usually involves women. The cops came a couple of times." Then more quietly she admitted, "We called them once." She looked around to make sure no one had heard. "It's not a great situation."

"No, it doesn't sound like it is." Tyler was confused about the many women, but he carried on. "Amazing what can go on behind closed doors in a quiet suburb like this one." Tyler rubbed his chin, pretending not to care too much. "So, rumor has it they had a child, huh?" Tyler pried, hoping to sound merely like a nosey parker.

"And with a maid, no less." Dick snorted.

Okay, so now we have a snob living beside a psycho murderer, thought Tyler. *Lovely neighborhood.*

"Well, as we said, we never saw a kid either, but you know, there's certainly a story there. Never a dull moment in West Heights." Dick smiled.

"You never know," Tyler added. He smiled and thanked them for their friendliness. He began backing away when he noticed that Becky was pointing behind him.

"I know there's a church a few blocks from here on Findlay Avenue. We don't go ourselves, but I've seen it there."

"Perfect. Thanks so much."

CHAPTER FIFTY-NINE
Tuesday, March 14th, 2020

Tyler called a taxi and waited for it at the intersection of Seventh Street and Marigold. He thought of Larsson having the cheek to say he worked at the pharmacy. *In two days, your little pharmacy will be responsible for the death of all life on this planet. Asshole.*

*

Diane's office was only a mile from the college, and as she often did, she met Westy for lunch. Before they both headed back to work, they took Westy's car and drove to Cynthia's apartment to drop off a bottle of wine and a note. She wasn't there, but her mother was. She looked frail and exhausted. They told her who they were and said they were thinking about the both of them during this difficult time. Her mom smiled and thanked them for their kindness.

They then decided to take a quick drive past Tyler's apartment. The Jeep was gone. He hadn't replied to any of their messages lately. They were worried all over again.

*

Tyler knew the next twenty-four hours would be the toughest part, but he was steadfast in his belief. It was for the greater good. Regardless of what happened to him, he knew what was at stake.

About three blocks from the Comfort Motel he found a local hardware store. He went to the hunting and fishing section and soon found a suitable twelve-inch hunting knife, similar to the one he had left up on Whisper Ridge. He also grabbed some large neoprene gloves. He paid cash and headed back to the motel for the night. It was time to mentally prepare for the morning.

CHAPTER SIXTY
Wednesday, March 15th, 2020

Cynthia's father passed away just before midnight. At Dr. Fortson's request, they had arrived at the hospice yesterday morning around ten and had not left his room since. They held her dad's hands as the nurses injected him with more and more pain medication. His breathing became labored. Soon his feet, followed by his legs, began to get very cold. Minutes before midnight, her dad took a few sudden and horribly disturbing gasps and began shaking. Then, just as suddenly, he went still.

Cynthia and her mom arrived back at her apartment just after four in the morning. She put her mom in her bed and rubbed her back until she had fallen asleep. Cynthia took a blanket out to her couch and lay down. She was still awake when the first light of dawn crept into the sky.

*

The taxi dropped him off a block away at 5:30 a.m. He paid cash, not once looking up at the driver. It was still relatively dark. He was wearing a black baseball hat, a black hoodie, and an old pair of jeans—all of which he had bought from the Salvation Army before leaving home.

He quickly trotted toward 337, taking a brief glance around. Once satisfied he had not been spotted, he sprinted to the side of the house and into the backyard, then knelt down against the back wall beside the man's bike.

On the other side of him was the window from which he had escaped. He knew the embalmed body of Mrs. Angel Larsson was sitting not twenty feet away. His heart was racing, and even in the crisp morning air, sweat prickled his skin.

The house was quiet. He half expected to hear The Sunny Skies and Smiles Trio music; however, all was deathly still. The wait was unbearable, but he wanted to be here before the neighborhood woke up.

*

At 7:45, he heard the front door open and then close. He pulled his hoodie over his head, held his knife tightly in his right hand, and moved toward the corner.

He had rehearsed this scenario a thousand times in his head. He would thrust the knife deep into Larsson's sternum as soon as he rounded the corner. He would then slice his throat, just to make sure. As horrific as it would be to carry out this act, he constantly reminded himself that it was for a higher cause. He had to do it. He had no choice—the lives of billions of people depended on him.

Tyler would then take off his hoodie and wrap it around the knife and gloves, bringing the evidence with him to be discarded back near the motel—far away from West Heights.

He would then walk nonchalantly south on Langer, rather than the way he came, just in case the neighbors came out again. He would call for a taxi as he walked. Arranging for it to meet him at the intersection of Seventh and Marigold.

When he got back to the motel, he would use a pay phone to call 911 and tell them a body could be found in the backyard of 337 Langer Road. He would also say they would want to go into the house, where they would find a girl upstairs in her bedroom. He would warn them that she cannot talk or see. Finally, they would want to check the basement. There they would come upon Mrs. Larsson sitting in her wedding dress and her head inside a plastic bag.

CHAPTER SIXTY-ONE
Wednesday, March 15th, 2020

Cynthia made coffee for herself and green tea for her mom. Though they never spoke of it, they both knew that they had been lucky to have been given a few days to say good-bye and grieve with her dad. This was a gift, and they would always treasure the stories, and even the laughter, that they were able to share with each other this past week.

Today Cynthia would head back to the hospice to sign papers and make some calls to let people know that her father, her rock, and her idol, was no longer with them.

CHAPTER SIXTY-TWO
Thursday, March 16th, 2020

Tyler's bus left at 9:00 a.m. He avoided watching the news in his motel room as he showered and got dressed. He felt surprisingly calm this morning. The thought of that monster being unable to harm anyone anymore reaffirmed that his actions were justified.

He grabbed a coffee on the way to the Cleveland Greyhound bus station, walking directly past the large garbage bin containing his hoodie wrapped around the knife and gloves. He didn't bat an eye.

*

The funeral would be held on Saturday. Her mother did not want to wait longer. Cynthia didn't expect a large crowd, though her dad had many connections in the community. She had already made arrangements on the phone with the funeral home and would visit the family lawyer today.

Now she needed to buy some pre-made nibbles for the reception that would follow the service. She was just walking into Good Foods when she saw Diane Branch.

Diane gave her a hug when Cynthia told her. She said that Westy and she would come to the funeral to show their support. Cynthia was overwhelmed by their generosity, considering they'd only briefly known each other. Their common bond was, of course, Tyler Stevens. A man missing in action yet again.

*

His bus ride was a blur. He was beginning to experience many conflicting emotions. Guilt would battle it out with righteousness. Feelings of justification would be challenged by those of horror, disgust, and remorse. Never had he purposefully killed anything larger than a fish before yesterday morning. Now he had slaughtered a human being with a hunting knife.

Tyler could still picture Larsson slowly falling to the ground and the look of surprise and confusion in his eyes, his red bicycle helmet tumbling onto the lawn as he reached out to try to get away.

Initially, Tyler felt at peace with his actions, especially considering it was now well past the hour of Armageddon. The world seemed to be continuing on as usual, *thank you very much*. However, the bus ride allowed him time to think. He began to question his own convictions, and he was now struggling. Killing a human can do that to you.

He also began to experience fear—but he had expected that. What he didn't expect was to be so paranoid about it. Did he leave a trace? Did someone check the garbage bin? Was his DNA all over the place? Was his "visiting my aunt" alibi airtight? He was getting very panicky, looking suspiciously at anyone who happened to glance his way. He was *way* too jittery.

By the time he reached Ann Arbor and walked into Alster Manor, he was an anxious wreck. Upon seeing her, Tyler wrapped his long arms around his aunt and refused to let go for the longest time. Eventually, the smell of her perfume and her warm embrace brought him relief. With her, he felt safe. When he finally did let go, he was crying.

Her room was quite large for a retirement home. The walls and bureaus were chockablock with pictures and keepsakes. She sat in her usual chair. Her gray hair was tied up neatly in a bun, and her thick glasses hung from a thin gold chain around her neck over her white blouse. She wore a cardigan around her shoulders.

Tyler pulled a stool next to her, again breathing in the familiar, comforting scent of her perfume. He'd made her tea, and now he sat near to her, holding her hand. As he always did when he visited, he had brought a sleeping bag. He would sleep on the floor beside her bed tonight and share stories, though he hoped to just listen tonight. He had nothing left.

His Aunt Del was his mom's older sister, by a whopping fifteen years. She was now pushing eighty and beginning to show it. Walking was harder for her these days, but her mind was still clear, and her appreciation for Tyler's visit was obvious.

Del and Blair Sherwood had never managed to have children of their own. Tyler had never known his Uncle Blair, as he had died of a brain aneurysm a year before the accident. Despite her own grief, his aunt had taken Tyler in and showered him with love, like he had always been her own.

She took the tea from him and smiled. "It's a special day today. Did you plan your visit on purpose?"

He cleared his throat, confused. "Special day?"

"Your sister's birthday, of course. The sixteenth. I was thinking recently that she would have been thirty-eight today. Imagine that."

Jesus, how could I have forgotten? March 16th was Tara's birthday.

"Of course, Mel," he lied. He had always called her Mel. It was his way of blending Mom and Del when he was young, and it stuck. She had always been both to him.

Tonight, Mel rubbed his hands between both of hers and told him all about her week, her aches and pains, her bridge club and library nights. By the time she had asked him about his own work, she found him leaning forward, head on the side of her chair, mouth wide open and fast asleep. She stroked his hair and began to sing some of his favorite lullabies.

CHAPTER SIXTY-THREE
Friday, March 17th, 2020

Cynthia went over the last details for tomorrow's ceremony. Her father had wanted to be cremated. His ashes scattered into the air outside of Missoula. He wanted them to fly high, on the wind—like a butterfly.

*

He'd had a rough sleep, even after climbing into his sleeping bag beside Mel's bed. His head was whirling, and his anxiety was heightening by the hour. He kept hearing knocking at the door and people in the corridor. He had to keep assuring himself it was just the staff working outside. He knew his paranoia was kicking in big-time, and he needed to get his head together.

He wanted to spend the morning chatting, walking, and just being with Mel; it was completely cathartic. Listening to the soothing tone and timbre of her voice brought back so many happy memories. He was in his safe place with her.

They ventured out to the gated garden behind Alster Manor. It was a beautiful spring morning, and they were alone. He could feel himself beginning to relax.

After twenty minutes of chitchat, Tyler decided he wanted to scratch a little deeper below the surface with Mel. He needed to learn more about his past. He had recently come to the realization that Mel was obviously not getting any younger. This had hit him hard, as he had never really imagined a world without her. She was the only real connection he had with his past, and he knew he had to savor these moments with her. It also helped distract him from his recent nefarious activities.

Tyler held Mel's arm and gently rubbed it with his hand as they walked. "Mel, we've never really talked much about my life before the accident."

Mel reflected on Tyler's comment for a moment. "No, I suppose we haven't."

"I mean, you told me all you could about Tara, Mom, and Dad. But not much about our life together—you know, as a family. What we did, what we loved to do together, and all that."

Mel nodded. She understood. "What would you like to know, honey?"

"Everything and anything." Tyler laughed and held her tight.

Mel spoke for an hour straight, recounting everything she could recall about Tyler's family and their lives together. She started with the earliest memories and worked her way up. They walked around and around the garden, arm in arm, and Tyler knew she was getting tired, but she said she was happy and insisted on continuing.

Mel had been so much older than his mom, but she had wanted to remain connected to her sister and her family and so had always inquired about their lives. Her memory was vivid. Because of this, she had many wonderful tales, and Mel was a marvelous storyteller. Tyler was entranced, and he felt calm returning to his body.

They sat down on one of the many benches for a while so Mel could rest. He asked her about his dad. Tyler had no memory of his father and, hence, very little emotional connection. He wanted to know so many things about him. *What were his dreams and ambitions? What did he want for me? What did his laughter sound like? How did he dress? What did Mom love most about him?* He asked Mel a million questions until he felt himself slowly reconnecting with his father's spirit.

He also wanted to know more about his sister, Tara. *Other than figure skating, what was she like at school? What television shows did she love? What were her birthday parties like every March 16th? Who had been invited?* Tyler had endless questions, and Mel graciously told him everything she could remember.

Tyler asked many of the same questions about his mom. Everything he heard seemed to give him meaning and a place in this world. Pieces of his family were living within him; they were part of who he was.

He wanted to hear about Mel's relationship with his mom. *What was it like having a sister fifteen years younger? Annoying? Fun? Did she make you proud or mad most of the time? And how did everyone get along in your family?* His curiosity seemed insatiable. Mel stood up and began walking again. Tyler joined her.

"Your mother was the beauty in the family, you know. I was always a bit jealous."

Tyler wrapped his arm through hers again as they continued on the pathway around the garden. He had always imagined his mother as a princess. "Hey, you're not so bad yourself, Mel."

"All three children were so different. I was the old conservative one, your mom was the beautiful and carefree one, and your uncle was—you know, the smart but volatile one."

Tyler could vaguely remember anyone talking much about his uncle. "Volatile?"

"You even called him Mean Uncle Gary."

"I did? Why?" Tyler was trying to picture his uncle.

"Well, as you know, his name was Dean Gary. Not sure why our parents called him that. Anyway, I guess you subconsciously changed it to Mean Gary after that summer you and your mom attempted to spend with him." Mel went quiet. She looked up at the trees. "I think the buds will be out soon."

Tyler was perplexed. *Attempted to spend with him?* He had no recollection of Mean Uncle Gary, nor of any summer spent with him.

"So he was the middle sibling, right? Mom was the youngest? I don't remember you mentioning much about him."

"Oh, Tyler, you're probably right. As I said, I spent so much darn time focusing on your future. The past was always so difficult for you."

Mel stopped and turned to face Tyler. She reached up and held his cheeks with both of her hands, looking directly in his eyes. "Oh, honey, after the accident, I wanted you to move forward."

Tyler smiled and wrapped his arms around her. "I understand. I appreciate that, Mel. You were amazing, what you did for me. I owe you everything."

After a moment, they walked on. "So why did I call him Mean Gary, Mel? Who was he mean to?"

Mel walked on in silence for a bit. "It was a long time ago, Tyler. My memory has faded somewhat with time."

"I understand."

"What I do recall was that you must have been quite young. I think it was the summer before the accident."

Tyler held her arm tight and absorbed every word Mel said. He wanted to hear everything about his past.

"Your father was doing a summer course in Detroit, an upgrade or something. He took Tara with him so she could attend some skating camps. Your mom thought it would be a good idea to take you to visit our brother for a few weeks during the summer holidays. You know, try to reconnect with him. Family was always very important to your mom."

Tyler tried to imagine his mom attempting to keep the family bonds tight. He loved that idea of her.

Mel stopped briefly to catch her breath, then continued to shuffle along. Tyler listened intently, wanting to soak in every single detail.

"To be honest, sadly your mom and I never really connected with him. Perhaps it was a girl-boy thing. Who knows? But that visit was her idea of a way to mend some fences. She wanted Dean Gary to get to know you, his nephew, and she was determined to give it a go."

The sun was now high in the sky, and the warm spring air felt soothing on their faces. "The first few days seemed to go okay. Dean Gary used to let you sit on his bike for a block or so in the mornings when he'd bike to work. You loved that." Mel looked up at Tyler and took a deep breath. "He then began to spend a lot of time with you after work. He built you a small fort in the basement. He had dress-up clothes…" Mel went quiet.

"What happened, Mel?"

Mel rubbed Tyler's arm and squeezed it. "He was always different, you know. And a leopard can't really change its spots."

Tyler realized he had really never thought of his uncle. He knew so little about him. "What do you mean? What happened, Mel?"

Mel kept walking, pulling Tyler along beside her. "Toward the end of August, your mom came home from shopping. He had dressed you up like a little girl. You had red lipstick smeared on your lips."

Tyler swallowed hard.

"It really frightened your mom, that did. Dean Gary was as high as a kite. He had access to a lot of drugs with his job, you know. They even took away his driver's license, which is why I think he still bikes to work to this day." Mel paused and lowered her voice. "Your mom got really worried and told him it wasn't right, the way he was playing with you down in that basement." Mel looked away briefly. "Then all hell broke loose."

Tyler took Mel's hand.

"You know, a crazy bachelor hosting a mother with a young boy wasn't really a good match from the outset. From what I remember your mom telling me, that same night he brought his part-time girlfriend home with him. I know my brother had been a little physical with some women in the past. He always had these tendencies, you know, with women. It kind of ostracized him from the family, to say the least. Anyway, there was lots of hitting and screaming that night."

Tyler swallowed again. He remained silent.

"My brother can get a little crazy from time to time. Your mom said he threatened both of you that night too."

Tyler tried to imagine a young mom trying to protect her child from her lunatic brother.

"Mean Gary," Tyler whispered to no one in particular.

They walked awhile longer in silence. Eventually, Tyler asked, "Why haven't I heard any of this before, Mel?"

Mel gave a little shrug. "As I said, call me silly, but I felt you had dealt with enough in your life. Too much for any one person. I thought it was always better to try to focus you on the future, you know?"

Tyler understood. Mel had always looked after him. He wanted to hear the rest of the story. "So what happened then?"

Mel stopped to take a few deep breaths and then continued. "You sure you want to hear this, honey?"

Tyler nodded.

"Your mom was a proud woman and a tough woman. She stood up to him that night, but as I said, he was high and irate. He was raging by then. They were yelling at each other and—he hit your mom. Knocked her over, right in front of you. You were crying, and she was crying. It was messy."

"He hurt Mom?" Tyler asked, his anger rising.

"She packed up the bags immediately and, with you in tow, left the house and headed down the street. Dean Gary was screaming behind her and throwing things at her from the door. As I said, he was a loose cannon. Probably still is."

Tyler tried to imagine the scene. Mom, bags, and a young son, running down the street. He was enraged that a brother could act like this to his sister and nephew.

"After that, she swore she would never go back to West Heights again. She never did."

Every fiber in Tyler's body froze.

"Are you okay, honey?" His aunt grabbed his arm and helped him to the small bench beside them. "Would you like some water or something?"

Tyler shook his head as he sat down. He must have heard her wrong. He cleared his throat. "I'm just a little tired. Did you say West Heights?"

Time stood still.

"Of course. It's not that far from here. Just a few hours. Dean Gary, your mom, and I all ended up staying within a few hours of where we were born. Heck, you were the adventurous one, heading west and becoming a fancy professor." Mel looked at him and said, "You sure you don't want some water?"

Tyler could feel the blood draining from his head and trickling down his spine. He was suddenly very cold, and he struggled to breathe.

Mel hugged him close to her and rubbed his arm. "Gosh, you're freezing. You okay, Tyler?"

He needed to know more. "Tell me more about Mean Gary. What happened next?" he managed to choke out.

"You sure? You don't look well."

Tyler nodded. "I'm sure." He was trying to find some context that made sense. His head was throbbing. *I had been to West Heights before.*

"I can still remember your mom telling me this story. She was so furious with our brother. First for beating up on Angel, that poor girlfriend of his—"

Tyler could feel his mind spinning. His chest was tight and squeezing in on itself; his entire world was shrinking.

"But mostly she was so upset for exposing you to that kind of behavior. And just as she was charging down the street, a man pulled up in his car."

Mel smiled, recalling her sister telling her about it. "The nice man leaned over and said, 'Margaret Coombs, is that really you?'" Mel looked over at Tyler. "Your mom loved telling this story. I must have told you this before."

"Go on," Tyler said softly. He was still trying to get over the West Heights bombshell.

"It turns out that the man in the car just happened to be one of her best friends from when she was at university. When she married your dad, they lost touch for a while but ended up reconnecting on occasion. Your dad really liked him too. She knew he lived in the area, but that was pretty amazing, don't you think?"

Tyler nodded and moved closer to his aunt.

"Well, can you imagine that? Holy mackerel, that day he was her knight in shining armor. He just so happened to live on the very same street as Dean Gary. Can you believe that?"

Tyler just listened, too emotionally exhausted to speak.

"Well, he invited you both to stay at his place. He lived alone, and he put you up for a couple of days. He was an army guy or something. Very gentlemanly. I think his name was David. David Summerland or something like that."

Tyler's stomach began to congeal. The tree branches swayed above him in the light breeze. "Sommerville?" he whispered softly, feeling dizzy.

"What? Oh, yes, that was it. Sommerville. See, I must have told you this story before."

"Mel," he said weakly, looking Mel in the eyes. "You don't happen to know Mean Gary's address offhand, do you?"

"What? Why?"

"Just because."

"Gosh, of course I do. Truth be told, I still try to write him, though he never writes back. I know he is a handful, and to think he is a professional pharmacist, no less. Still, I am the only family he has left, I suppose."

Tyler was numb. "What is it, Mel?"

"The address? It's 337 Langer Road, West Heights, Ohio. Though I can't recall the postal code."

Tyler slowly turned and stared at the fence ahead of him. He was sinking in quicksand. "And this David Sommerville lived on the same street, right?" Tyler could still see Sommerville's skeleton grabbing the gas mask at the top of his stairs.

"That's right. Crazy, isn't it?"

There was no sense in stopping now. "He was a golfer." *Might as well throw more chum into the water. The sharks are already circling.*

"Yes, I think he was, Tyler. My, what a good memory you have. See, I did tell you this before." Mel was smiling and hugging him tightly.

Tyler kept looking ahead. Motionless. It was all becoming clear. "Mel, have you ever heard of a band called The Sunny Skies and Smiles Trio?"

"Oh gosh, Tyler. I can't believe you of all people are asking me that question!" She looked over at him in disbelief. "Are you serious?"

Tyler didn't respond. He was limp.

"You listened to it pretty much nonstop after the accident. I can still sing all those songs to this day. All those silly songs about dungarees and bunnies, and all those jokes." Mel smiled and continued. "When you were both young, you and your sister used to sing one of the songs from that album over and over, giggling and chasing each other around the room. I can still hear it to this day." Mel started to sing the chorus of "This Train Is Bound for Glory."

Tyler looked up at the trees. She was right. The buds were starting to come out.

"After your sister died, you used to lie down in front of the stereo and listen to it while cuddling our old ginger tabby. Do you remember him, Tyler? Tangerine? You could never pronounce Tangerine, though. You called him Tanger for short. So cute."

Tyler closed his eyes. He felt dizzy.

Mel was silent for a while, and Tyler sensed her confusion. "Why do you ask about The Sunny Skies and Smiles Trio?" Mel asked.

Tyler was just holding on. "Tell me, Mel." His voice was weak now. "What does Borden mean to you?"

"Borden? I'm not sure—or do you mean Camp Borden?"

Tyler didn't respond.

"Gosh, Tyler, I thought we almost lost you too."

"Lost me?" he whispered. He forced himself to open his eyes.

"Borden was the camp up north that I sent you to the summer after the accident. I thought you would benefit from the change of scenery."

Tyler wrapped his arms in front of him and hugged himself tight. He was beginning to remember.

"But after only two days, you became really sick. I mean really sick. I got a call. They said you had contracted some kind of virus, and they needed me to come immediately. By the time I got there, they had already taken you to the local hospital to run tests. They hooked you up to an IV right away."

Tyler could see a flock of birds circling above him. They seemed unsure of which way to go.

"They had no clue what it was. You were in pretty rough shape. They kept you there for seven days. Imagine that, seven whole days." Mel shook her head. "I was so worried. I was also riddled with guilt for sending you there in the first place, especially after all you had been through."

Tyler wanted to purge; his entire body felt like it was floating. "Can we go back to the room, Mel? I'm feeling pretty tired. I need to rest."

Mel checked her watch. It was only 11:30. Tyler looked pale and was shaking. "Tyler, do you want me to call you a doctor? We have lots around here." She was distraught.

Tyler shook his head. "No, I just need to lie down for a bit."

When they returned to her room, she watched him crawl into the sleeping bag by her bed. She sat in her chair, watching him. "Can I get you anything, honey?"

I just want to curl up and fade away. "I just need to rest, Mel."

Tyler stared vacantly at the wall in front of him. On a shelf above her television, there were some framed pictures. Most were of her and her husband, Blair. There was one of his mom, Mel, and Dean Gary when they were very young.

To the right, there was a picture of his own family. The four of them were obviously off to one of his sister's figure skating competitions. He was wearing a sweater and bright yellow mittens. His sister was dressed in her figure skating outfit. A blue skirt, a white top, and pink ribbons in her hair. Tara had a goofy grin on her face. His parents stood behind them, smiling proudly. He recognized the silver locket around his mother's neck.

"Mel," Tyler asked weakly.

"Yes, Tyler."

"Who is Elias Larsson?"

Mel did not respond immediately. "Why, Tyler?"

"I just need to know."

"Well, I'm sure you do know, honey."

He was too tired to think. "Please tell me, Mel."

His aunt crossed her arms in front of her and took a deep breath. "Well, honey, that's the boy that was driving."

"Driving?" Tyler whispered.

"That night he had been drinking. He was only a teenager. It is all so tragic, honey. You were so young."

Tyler closed his eyes. He could feel everything beginning to implode. He was falling down a deep, dark tunnel. He managed to crawl out of his sleeping bag and make his way on his hands and knees to where his aunt was sitting. He put his head on her lap and wrapped his arms around her. He started to cry.

Mel slowly stroked his hair. "Oh, honey, I know it's still so hard for you."

He was utterly empty. He cried until he had nothing left. He felt as though he was a young boy again. A boy whose world was disappearing around him.

Eventually, he managed to lift his head and look up at his aunt. "Mel?" Tyler whispered, tears rolling down his cheeks.

"Yes, honey?"

"I have to go home tomorrow morning."

"I know, Tyler." She continued to hold him tight.

"I may not be able to see you again for a long time."

"I know you are a busy man. Imagine you being a professor at that fancy university! I'm so proud of you, Tyler." Mel smiled and gave him a squeeze. "It will be good to see you whenever you can spare the time, honey."

CHAPTER SIXTY-FOUR
Saturday, March 18th, 2020

Tyler somehow just managed to make the half-past eleven Delta flight out of Ann Arbor the next morning. He was at his apartment in Missoula by late afternoon. It was all he could do to stumble his way up the steep stairs and unlock his door. He collapsed on the floor in his kitchen.

Tyler's mind was now merely a wasteland, and he could barely function. He had been running on fumes for too long. Lying on his back on the floor, he managed to pull the cell phone out of his pocket and press Cynthia's number.

He was sent directly to her voicemail. He closed his eyes.

"It's Tyler. I think I've done a bad thing."

*

Nearly a hundred people had attended the memorial service for the most amazing father anyone could have ever asked for. Cynthia was a wreck, but she held on, thanks to people like Westy and Diane, who had rolled up their sleeves and chipped in to help with the reception afterward. They handed out sandwiches and tea and were simply there for her.

It was only later that evening when Cynthia was heading to bed that she was able to check her voicemail. Her heart went cold.

CHAPTER SIXTY-FIVE
Sunday, March 19th, 2020

The morning sun streamed through the windows as Tyler lay in bed looking out at the Bitterroot Range. He hadn't slept all night. His head was a pool of swirling visions, all surging and crashing against every region of his brain. He had lost all ability to function effectively.

Like a blitzkrieg, it descended on him and completely overwhelmed his consciousness, and there was no defense against the onslaught. He tried to focus and recalibrate but to no avail. He tried desperately to find an explanation. There was none.

*

Sheriff Patychuk received an odd call from someone at the FBI satellite office in Bozeman. It was about an incident in Ohio. They claimed that a Missoula resident may know something about a homicide in a Cleveland suburb, and they needed his team to check on his whereabouts.

They said they'd used some facial recognition software to compile security footage from various locales and then search for a match within their database. "With people dangling their dicks all over social media these days, it's pretty easy to connect the dots," the man had explained. "Amazing how quickly that shit works, huh?" he had bragged.

The man had alluded that it was early stages, of course, so confidentiality needed to be assumed. Seems the suspect visited some areas of interest, you know, bus stations, hardware stores, and places like that. Had the good sheriff ever heard of a Tyler Stevens? He was a professor at Missoula College.

"Well, I'll be damned," Patychuk had muttered.

The sheriff's reaction told the man on the other end of the line everything he needed to know.

"Perhaps you can swing by his place and bring him in for some questioning? We can be there in the morning. Call me directly at this number when you know anything."

CHAPTER SIXTY-SIX
Sunday, March 19th, 2020

C ynthia knew she could not return Tyler's call. She also knew that he had been reaching out for help, but she was not the person to give it.

What bad thing did you do, Tyler? Cynthia thought, deciding instead to let Westy and Diane know that he had called and that he seemed distressed and desperate.

Westy thanked her for the call and tried to phone Tyler. There was no answer.

*

The *Cleveland Plain Dealer*'s initial blurb about the murder would run in the morning. They didn't have much information yet, only that the body of a local pharmacist, Dr.

Dean Gary Coombs, was found in his backyard in West Heights.

Police had said they received an anonymous call informing them where to find the body. They also were told to search the house for other possible victims, but as of now, no other people had been found. Dr. Coombs lived alone at 337 Langer Road in West Heights.

*

Sheriff Patychuk and three deputies arrived at Tyler's apartment just shortly after noon. His Jeep was parked in the driveway. One officer waited by it while the others carefully climbed the stairs.

They would inform Mr. Stevens that he would be required to accompany them for some questioning. Questions about an incident that occurred in West Heights, Ohio, on March 15th. They wouldn't mention to him that the FBI would also be joining the meeting.

PART SIX

Figment

CHAPTER SIXTY-SEVEN

N ine days after Tyler had been taken into custody, Cynthia had been summoned by Sheriff Patychuk to meet with members of the FBI in his office at the precinct.

Since Tyler had officially been a client of Dr. Chan's before the death of Dr. Dean Gary Coombs, and since he was now a suspect in a murder investigation, they wanted to know why she had referred him elsewhere. More specifically, why did she decide to recommend a more sophisticated kind of treatment immediately prior to the event that occurred in West Heights, Ohio? What they were really asking was, did she have prior knowledge or suspicion of Tyler's impending act of violence against his uncle?

The two agents listened to Dr. Chan's long and strange account of her many conversations with Professor Stevens. Much of it seemed to jibe with what they had uncovered in his apartment. The surveillance cameras were still operational, and they found his camping equipment piled near the front door.

On his computer was a treasure trove of information that suggested intent. His internet searches, while confusing, were definitely focused on West Heights. They wanted to know if she had been aware of his keen interest in virology. Or in people named Elias and Angel Larsson? She told them she had no knowledge of any of these things.

The FBI had done some pretty quick work. They had discovered a return flight purchase to Ann Arbor, Michigan, which the airline confirmed Tyler Stevens had taken. There had been a bank withdrawal of nearly two thousand dollars two nights before his flight and an ATM withdrawal of five hundred dollars the evening before he left town.

Dr. Coombs's talkative neighbors, Dick and Becky Shore, had identified Tyler Stevens from a picture they were shown. They claimed it was the same man who had been talking with them and Dr. Coombs the day before the attack. He had been looking for a church for his wife and daughter. But he had seemed to be very interested in Dr. Coombs.

The Cleveland taxi services confirmed the drop-off in West Heights of a single passenger on two consecutive days, March 14th and 15th. Similarly, the West Heights taxi company confirmed two pickups at Marigold and Seventh Street later on those same days. It seemed Mr. Stevens was unaware that all taxis in the Cleveland area were equipped with cameras.

This location was only a few blocks from the residence of Dr. Dean Gary Coombs. Both pickups in Cleveland occurred just outside of the Comfort Motel, the same location where a single passenger was delivered on both days.

Surveillance camera footage acquired from Donny's Hardware in Cleveland showed a man that looked like Tyler Stevens walking down the aisles of the hunting and fishing department. He was wearing a ball cap, but there were some pretty clear pictures of his face.

They had evidence of a cash purchase by what appeared to be the same man in the video. He had bought a pair of neoprene gloves and a hunting knife whose serrated edge and blade length was, according to the coroner's report, consistent with the weapon used in the Coombs attack.

Similar surveillance footage was gathered from a coffee shop, the lobby of the Comfort Motel, and both inside and outside the Cleveland Greyhound bus station. Facial recognition software found a 99 percent match based on Mr. Tyler Stevens's social media and professional postings.

Clearly the perpetrator was not a seasoned criminal.

CHAPTER SIXTY-EIGHT

By the end of the month, the media circus had descended on Missoula. It didn't take much to cause a stir in such a small community. Missoula College had banned reporters from the campus, but it was hard to escape them. The gossip machine was in high gear.

The entire city seemed to have an opinion about how and why this professor would have wanted to murder his own uncle, a man he had never really known. Everywhere was rife with the sensational story.

Westy and Diane had been subpoenaed and were going to have to testify at the upcoming trial. They knew it was going to be heartrending to get through. They knew they would have to recount, in a very public way, all the details of their conversations with Tyler. Everyone would listen in disbelief as Diane and Westy described Tyler's fantastic stories of phantom photographs that no one else could see. They would *ooh* and *ahh* when hearing about the strange communications that had allegedly appeared on Tyler's phone, not to mention the various radio and television episodes. The thought of having to share all of this made them both feel sick. While the town was fascinated, they were devastated.

The had just arrived at the courthouse and were halfway up the stairs that led toward the front doors when a very determined-looking male reporter started sprinting toward Diane and Westy. "Excuse me, Mr. Westaway, may I ask you a few questions?"

A crowd soon followed. In an instant, people began swarming in as they saw what was happening. Cameras, phones, and microphones seemed to come out of nowhere. Within seconds, the couple's path was blocked. "Excuse me, sir, how well did you know Mr. Stevens?" The man pushed closer, causing the others to do likewise, each jockeying for a prime position.

Then from their right, a woman pressed her cell phone in front of Diane's face, attempting to record the encounter. "Ms. Branch, is it true you knew the accused and were aware of his desire to murder his uncle?"

Diane grabbed Westy's hand, and together they attempted to maneuver around the surging crowd.

"Why did you not report him to the police?" another voice yelled from the din. Mercifully, a courthouse security officer arrived and gradually was able to secure a path for them to continue into the building.

CHAPTER SIXTY-NINE

"Hello, Mrs. Sherwood?"

"Hello? Who is this, please?"

"Mrs. Sherwood, it's Cynthia Chan, Tyler's friend. I called you several months ago. I don't know if you remember me?"

There was a short silence. "Yes, I do."

"Mrs. Sherwood, I just wanted to call to see how you were doing. This must all be so horrible for you."

There was another pause. "It is." Mel's voice was fragile. She sounded defeated.

"Is there anything I can do for you?"

"Tell them to stop bothering me. So many questions…"

"I understand, Mrs. Sherwood. They're only trying to do their job."

"I don't have anyone anymore, you know. No parents, no siblings. Now I don't even have my Tyler." Her voice was almost inaudible.

Cynthia told her that she knew what she was going through. She left her number and told her to call her if she ever wanted to talk.

EPILOGUE
Mid-August

Westy's truck easily handled the bumpy logging roads below the Bitterroot Mountains. Diane was beside him and had the GPS on her phone locked and loaded, guiding him down the series of unused roads and finally telling him to pull over just before the first narrow jammer road.

They helped each other with their backpacks, checked their coordinates, then began walking. Forty-five minutes later, they reached their destination. It was still relatively early in the morning, yet it was already hot. They both took a long drink of water. They decided to rest a few minutes before starting their ascent. It was going to be a ballbuster, but they needed to do this.

By midafternoon, the terrain began to level off. They found a small clearing where they collapsed in silence for a rest. They were both exhausted. They were fit, but not "Tyler fit."

After twenty minutes, some energy bars, and lots of water, Diane checked her compass, and they continued on their way. In a few minutes, they found a deer trail that seemed to be heading in the right direction. They followed it.

Thirty minutes later, the foliage opened up, and they could see a small pond with a beautiful vista of the valley beyond. They both smiled and walked the last few feet.

They dropped their packs off beside the first log they found, seeing remnants of an old fire pit beside it. They knew this must be the spot.

*

Westy and Diane spent the rest of the afternoon walking around the pond and marveling at the view of the valley. It was a simply beautiful day, and the sun glistened off the sparkling water. The wildflowers seemed to be bursting with color, spinning and dancing in the gentle breeze.

Westy started a small fire using some of the twigs and small logs he found scattered around the old fire pit. They must have been left there by Tyler. Diane looked around and noticed some fur limbs on the ground and guessed that was where he had put his tent last winter. As it was the only flat area in the vicinity, she decided it would be an excellent place to put theirs as well.

While Westy cooked, Diane sat on the log, watching the sun disappear behind the trees on the western side of the pond. She couldn't get over how magical it was. The air was cool, but it was a spectacular evening.

Both Diane and Westy had discussed it at length and agreed that they would come here as a tribute to their friend Tyler Stevens. They loved Tyler and missed him desperately. It seemed to be the right thing to do.

They knew that Tyler was ill now, and, like with any illness, it was becoming harder to remember him as he was before. Though they understood the old Tyler was no longer with them, they refused to let that tarnish the memory of their friend.

After they finished dinner, Westy pulled out a bottle of Malbec that he had hidden in his pack and lugged up the mountain. It was for Tyler, after all.

He filled their metal mugs to the rim, and they both leaned back against the log, raising a toast to their friend. They held each other tight and sat in silence, watching as the first stars lifted above the horizon.

*

Back in Missoula, Cynthia had already formulated a plan. She would be taking time off this fall to be with her mother. They were both lonely and needed something to look forward to. It was time to do something about it.

She had approached her mom with the idea of a road trip across the country. Missoula to New York and back. It would take nearly a month, but it would be the adventure they both needed. Her mom seemed excited, so Cynthia got down to organizing it.

She had already decided that they would take a small detour to Ann Arbor, Michigan. She had a feeling her mom would get on well with Mrs. Sherwood.

*

The morning sun took a while to hit Whisper Ridge, and by the time it did, Westy and Diane had already packed up their gear in preparation for leaving. Westy walked down to the pond, wanting to take a few last pictures while the light was good. Diane took advantage of the silent, peaceful morning to reminisce about Tyler and all the wonderful times they had shared.

She walked past the fire toward a grove of alders. Diane remembered Tyler talking about that strange picture he had received after his first time up to Whisper Ridge. He claimed it had been taken from the other side of the fire. *Perhaps from these alders?*

She remembered how frightened he had seemed when he first realized he was having these hallucinations. They had hugged and cried together. His body had heaved as he sobbed with fear.

She was just about to turn back when her eyes caught a glimpse of something. It was about five feet beyond the first few alders. She almost hadn't noticed it.

Diane crouched down beneath the limbs, slowly moving toward what appeared to be some kind of small faded backpack.

She was going to call out to Westy, but he was already on the other side of the pond. She moved closer and knelt down. Despite its weathered condition, she immediately recognized it as Tyler's. It was his daypack.

There was a curious, dense grove of trees just past the pack. It seemed to almost shimmer and was oddly dark.

The trees above were beginning to sway slightly, and a cold breeze whirled around her. It felt strange there, as if something was lurking. Diane shivered and grabbed the pack, then hurried back to the campsite.

Diane could see Westy was on his way back. She called out to him, holding the pack above her head. When he eventually reached her side, they both sat down together on the log.

"Tyler's pack," Westy whispered; he recognized it as well. Though a little worse for wear, it was easily identifiable. He noticed dark stains on the pack beneath the straps. It looked like dried blood.

He watched as Diane undid the tie on the top. "Must have been out here all winter." She opened up the small pack and peered in. She looked briefly at Westy, took a breath, and then stuck her hand inside.

The first thing she felt was a pair of binoculars. She pulled them out. They both felt a sudden rush of sadness. They had seen Tyler use these binoculars many times. Westy put his arm around Diane and gently pulled her toward him.

Diane reached into the pack again and carefully pulled out Tyler's large hunting knife. Though neither of them mentioned it, they both thought of Tyler's uncle. He had been killed by a similar kind of hunting knife. She placed it on the log beside the binoculars.

Finally, she pulled out the narrow flashlight. They both looked at each other. It was hard to describe the emptiness they both felt at that moment. They put everything back in the pack. It was time to go.

Westy strapped Tyler's daypack to the top of his own pack. He then flung the entire load up onto his shoulders and began following Diane down the deer trail. They were heading home.

Westy had no way of noticing it slipping out of the top of Tyler's daypack behind him.

And even as they disappeared into the woods, the small pink ribbon was still spinning and twirling in the gentle breeze, slowly falling toward the ground. Almost like a butterfly.

Don't forget to leave a review! And if you want more check out C.W Johnston at www.cwjohnston.com

Acknowledgements

I'd like to thank the following people: Kate, Emily, and Sammy for their support. Pam Jolliffe and Julian Lees for their early edits, contribution of time, and sage advice. To Bronwen Jervis and Brian Carr for their beta-reads. And finally, to my editor, Kate Schomaker for inspiring me to be better.

About the Author

Clayton Johnston lives with his wife on Vancouver Island, in beautiful British Columbia, Canada. He first started writing in his 20s on Harbour Island in the Bahamas where he began his teaching career. After purchasing his first computer he typed his first of many stories while his young daughter sat in his lap. Now with two grown daughters, a job that has taken him to over 65 countries around the world, he spends most of his free time writing. Figment is his first novel. You can find him tweeting as @Real_CWJohnston or taking pictures on Instagram @c.w..johnston. You can also visit his official Facebook page at @cwjohnston60 and website at www.cwjohnston.com

Figment

Made in the USA
Monee, IL
20 March 2023